AFTER THE VIRUS

Library and Archives Canada
Doidge, Meghan Ciana, 1973 —
After The Virus/Meghan Ciana Doidge — Paperback
ISBN 978-0-9876851-8-6

Cover illustration by Intrlight
Cover Design by Eternal Geekery

AFTER THE THE VIRUS

MEGHAN CIANA DOIDGE

AUTHOR'S NOTE: CONTENT

While After the Virus is fundamentally a love story (on multiple levels) it is also a horror/post-apocalyptic/dystopian standalone novel with all the graphic violence, general psychotic behaviour (not main characters), and ongoing traumatic situations that setting implies.

Content of Note (not exhaustive): violence (on the page), including assault, attempted murder, murder, blood, death, and gore, explicit language, attempted sexual assault (not between main characters), discussions/thoughts of past abuse, kidnapping and hostage situations (main character and a child), plague (aftermath of) and weaponized zombie-like creatures. Sexual situations but no explicit sex scenes. **Adult 18+**

Content of note and a list of tropes can also be found on MCD's website: www.madebymeghan.ca/after-the-virus

After the virus decimates 99.9% of the world's population and all traces of humanity along with it, Rhiannon and Will are forced to move beyond their past fame, fortune, and personal demons to rescue a mute girl from the clutches of two warring cults.

1 / HER

WAKING UP WAS NEVER A GOOD IDEA, AND THIS morning she had momentarily thought she was ... before, before them, before this life. If this was what it was to survive the virus, she didn't much like it, but the alternative, killing herself, seemed cheap and easy.

She could hear a woman weeping, something she hadn't ever done. *Shut the fuck up, you'll just entice them*: the walking horrors and their keepers.

They hadn't raped her ... yet. They had other plans.

If you weren't for breeding, they fed you to the Infected; that was how they kept them alive, inhumanly strong and terrifying — the blood of the immune.

It felt like months, but she was sure she had only been here a few days. She was also very sure her friends-of-necessity were dead.

It was difficult to gauge in the dark. They, all women, were crammed into some concrete box, not chained but definitely trapped. There was a toilet; the door had been removed and it didn't flush, but at least they weren't continually sitting in piss and shit.

She was definitely in some city they were working to get back online, but food still came in cans.

There'd been a power surge yesterday, and when her eyes adjusted, she'd seen the door through which she would find freedom or death.

Chairlike cages, stirrups, and women with electrodes to their heads and bellies — baby mills? They made sure she had seen it all, like they were giving her some sort of insanity tour when they dragged her in.

She was either going to go crazy, die of boredom, or kill the woman who kept trying to fiddle her whenever she succumbed to sleep.

Footsteps.

She could also hear the chains they kept around the Infecteds' necks. *Why bring them at all?* These few women were too broken to bolt.

They came every few hours to either take women or drop new cattle. Normally, along with all the others, she pressed against a gritty wall, eyes downcast, willing them not to see her.

Not today.

Today, when she heard the bolts sliding, she stood and, stumbling over scrambling bodies, moved to the very center of the sty. Trapped here, she was losing all sense of being. It was time to make her stand. It was time to try to get through that door. She'd rather be dead than immobile.

She'd been told, before this, that she was beautiful, that her eyes were striking, so she ran her fingers through her hair and tilted her head. Harsh light struck her eyes, but she struggled to keep them wide, perhaps even coy, if she could remember how to be so. Silence fell, and even more so than before, she felt their stares.

Two men loomed in the doorway with — heard more

than seen — one of them. The Infected, all chain-rattling and snuffling great gobs of green snot. There had to be an ever-present danger of the hunter mutinying against the master — they didn't even keep the chains taut — but right now, she didn't give a fuck about anyone's life but her own.

"Hello, sweet thang," he, with the shotgun, purred. "Remember me?"

Over his shoulder, the Infected groaned in an odd, soft sort of pleasure at the smell of so many of the Immune so near.

She wouldn't reply, not to him, not as if he had a soul, but she did suck on her lower lip to strike a thinking pose and keep them distracted.

Yeah, asshole, I remember. Your dick is so insignificant you use a shotgun instead. She wouldn't scream, so you pulled the trigger three times.

"We were just coming to get ya. Lucky girl. The Boss wants a taste, so no chains and chair for you. You get to ride the biblical way."

Great, he thinks he's funny — maybe even charming — but the fucking prick screamed his own name as he jizzed all over that fucking shotgun.

They reached for her, but she stepped forward so their fingers just brushed her bare arms.

The Infected growled at her nearness.

She dropped her eyes. She hadn't been this close to one since... since it was someone she had known before. It reeked, worse for having been dying for months.

"Look out, sweet," Asshole cautioned. "Any bites out of you the Boss wants, he'll take." The two of them yanked harshly on the Infected's neck chain.

What the fuck was his name? She couldn't remember

and she wanted to shriek it in triumph when she bludgeoned him with his own shotgun.

Their caution hinted that they wouldn't hurt her, not too badly, unless forced. A woman was rare. A woman of childbearing age was precious. So her full lips and wide hips would keep her relatively safe, until... Well, there wasn't going to be an until, not like this, not here, not if she could do anything about it.

They guided her down a concrete hall. She could hear generators whirling nearby, but didn't see what they powered. Shadowed stairs led up. She could smell dampness, not the ever-present seeping rusty water mixed with piss and puke, but actual fresh rain.

The stairs led out. Outside.

She swallowed her hope so they didn't feel her energy blooming. *How much of the city did they control? All of it?* If so, she was fucked.

More men at the top of the stairs equaled more staring. She hoped their boss scared them dickless; otherwise she'd miscalculated. She could already feel pricks coming to attention, ready and willing to plunder her abyss. Except the Infected, of course; it just wanted to eat her.

She paused to consider that she might be crazy. She'd been in her head for days now. *What if this is all some sort of massive psychosis brought on from some brain tumor?* But then she quickly discarded this theory as unhelpful and irrelevant. It wasn't like this was some movie, and even if it was all in her head, she still had to be herself and react like she would. She still had to be in control.

They reached for her because she'd stopped, so she jerked away. They laughed. *Men. Laughing.* The virus had really shit-kicked women's lib. She hadn't grown up with four brothers not knowing how to handle a man. They were dogs and she was nobody's bitch. Her bite was worse.

Cool air lifted her hair; she breathed like she hadn't had oxygen for days, and looked to see that they were in a glassed space, like an atrium. It was night. More underlings held the door open expectantly, so she headed that way. Outside, the street was wet enough to reflect the moon.

The Infected, already highly riled, lunged at the door guys as it followed her. They'd been stupid enough to lean in as she'd passed by, perhaps hoping for some contact, perhaps hoping for a whiff or a smile.

Shotgun Asshole got tangled in its chain.

Yelling and beating commenced. The Infected roared in response even as it tried to cower between the neglected dried husks of the indoor palm trees.

The street was empty.

She felt the sure grip of her Merrell soles as she sprang ahead, and was fucking glad she'd salvaged them from an outlet mall only days before they captured her.

These men had grown accustomed to, and lazy with, their dominance. She was a hundred feet away before they gave chase. She hit side streets and turned often.

The Infected could track her, of course. It loved a hunt.

She darted into an alley where they had obviously been clearing cars, though they hadn't bothered dealing with the rotting corpses. She forced her brain to see these just as obstacles to be climbed and dodged. If her hand sank into some soggy chest cavity or her ankle twisted in mushed brains, she just ignored it. Her heart beat firmly in survival mode.

As she hit a relatively cleared section, some other person or people cut across her path — perhaps deliberately — twice.

The effort to breathe quietly used too much air. She couldn't soften the slap of her shoes on the wet concrete. She wasn't going to make it.

She pressed behind a dumpster to listen to the chase. The men and the bellowing Infected were a couple of streets off as best as she could gauge in the dark confusion. She pondered that she hadn't seen any dead bodies for a couple of streets now, but then chided herself to focus.

"Left, left, and right," a voice cut through her labored breathing. She tried listening to source him in the dark, but stopping breathing wasn't currently an option. *Was that heavily shadowed brick doorway concealing someone?* The darkness was too deep to be sure. "Go," he insisted. Someone else darted from the doorway and headed right.

She ran left.

"I see her, heading towards the park," a woman, from a window above and behind her, yelled.

Needing to trust the first voice, she veered left again and then right. A tall chain-link fence, pushed by unseen hands, suddenly closed the alley behind her.

There were people here. People helping her escape. Her brain clicked from image to image. The crisscrossing of her path had been to confuse the hunter, to whom any immune blood beckoned. Then the guiding voice and now the gate, but she couldn't seek haven, couldn't risk that this new group wasn't just like all the others had been. The disintegration of humanity seemed utterly complete.

She continued to run through alleys and back lanes until she realized she was completely alone and compelled to stop. She tucked into some shadows. Her stomach revolted; nothing came up.

She might have passed out there. If so, that wasn't good because she wasn't sure how much lead time she'd lost. But then she heard barking.

Savage barking. A dog. Here? She'd only seen maggot-ridden corpses in yards and ditches since... since everyone who was going to die had. She instinctively followed the barks.

The barks led in a direction she knew she shouldn't go, but the dog's pain and desperation drew her, and then ... then she heard the laughter.

More men. Laughing.

Before she even located them, she picked up a heavy piece of metal, some rusted length of plumbing that had deadly weight. Turning the corner, she found them clustered in a basketball court nestled between derelict high-rises.

They were baiting the dog, a powerful Rottweiler, against one of the Infected. *Fuck, how many were they keeping alive?* One less, if she had her way.

The dog is fatally hurt, her brain argued. *You aren't going to save it, even if you sacrifice yourself.* But her feet kept moving.

She smashed the pipe down to split the nearest head, and then on the reverse stroke, probably sent nose-bone shards into a second brain.

In the following confusion, she flipped the pipe length-wise and drove it into the Infected's back. Their skin was saggy, soft, a bit like butter.

She easily skewered its heart.

In its dying rage, it grabbed the nearest man and tore off an arm.

Clawing hands were all over her now.

"Fuck, hold her!"

By the screams, it sounded like the Infected was eating one of them, but two others had her down.

Her skull smacked the pavement.

Blackness engulfed.

She realized they were trying to undo her jeans. Her self-rigged chastity belt was holding them off, but not for long.

Though she'd lost the pipe, she lashed out with fists and feet and received another blow to the head. But the dog wasn't out of the fight, and it tore at the throat of the one on top of her.

With her upper body freed, she managed to smash her heel through the teeth of the one on her legs, and she was up, slipping in the blood, fleeing, once again, for her life.

After a block, she chanced a look back. They weren't following, but the dog was, barely. With each stride she took, it fell farther back.

She couldn't stop. She could hear them shouting into walkie-talkies, and the Infected's dying bellows. They'd be reinforced and all over her soon.

The dog went down, then managed to get up again. Its left flank was torn, the skin dragging, and maybe the leg was broken or dislocated.

Even in this dark, they'd be able to follow the blood trail.

So with her brain warring with something she hesitated to identify as her heart, she stopped and turned back.

The dog made it a few more feet before collapsing: down for good.

"Hey, love." Her voice sounded harsh and she flinched. "I've got you, do you trust me?" *Weren't Rotties supposed to average a hundred pounds? Though this one was terribly emaciated, so maybe — Fuck. Don't fucking think, just do, Rhiannon.*

She approached. The dog laid down its head, and, taking that as submission and acceptance, she hunkered down and somehow rolled it into a fireman's lift and up.

With the dog across her shoulders, she took a step. "We can do it: first a pharmacy, then food." She always felt better with a solid script to follow.

She smiled, the feeling of which was foreign and freeing.

HE WASN'T TOO SURE HOW MANY BODIES HE'D lifted onto the pyre, but he was damn sure they weren't going to burn like well-aged firewood.

Course, he'd never burned a body before.

He didn't count. Didn't want to count. He'd done everything he could before he'd dealt with the bodies. Cleared the cars, boarded windows, even swept the main street.

There weren't more than thirty houses in the township, but they'd been prolific people. The bodies of the children particularly bothered him.

He wasn't one of them originally, but he thought they might have accepted him eventually despite the twang in his accent and his permanent tan. He'd never know now; every last one of them was dead or, if there had been survivors, they hadn't stuck around.

He didn't mind the quiet.

His life before hadn't been so labor intensive, though he'd painted his father's house one summer during high school: brown with brown trim. It still bothered him, not using a contrast color for the trim. Course, it didn't much matter; who knew if the house was even still standing?

But he enjoyed feeling his muscles stretch under his skin. He felt powerful here; this town was something he could control among the chaos.

It was getting warmer, so he had needed to deal with the bodies. He was pretty sure that "immune to the virus" didn't mean immune to everything, and he wasn't interested in dying because he'd been too much of a coward to clean.

He didn't like to think about immunity, because that just brought up thoughts of self-worth and why he was still here when others weren't.

Others. What a nothing of a word to use, even in his own head. People. People who he'd never loved, couldn't love, like they'd deserved.

He stopped shifting bodies. He'd tied them all, one by one, in sheets from the homes he found them in, hoping that they wouldn't break apart too badly on the way to the fire. The back of the pickup was almost empty. It wasn't time for a break, but he could feel the darkness pulling him.

He cracked a can of cola, Coke, of course, though he couldn't really tell you the difference. The bubbles always somehow lightened his mood.

He'd spent months dwelling, wallowing in wretchedness, hopping from survivor group to survivor group, until all the dead had finally died.

All the wants, needs, and desires of all the other Immune, even though so few of them remained, crowded and controlled his own.

He grew tired of not knowing which woman had crawled into his sleeping bag and, come morning, the tense grins from their chosen mates. As far as he knew, he never impregnated any of them. Their need to breed when surrounded by death was almost instinctual, but it wasn't his instinct. Their eyes grew dim and sunken as each month passed. Hunger gnawed more than bellies.

When spring made mountains passable, he'd moved on from the final group. He thought they'd been sorry to see him go, his able body and all.

He crushed the empty pop can, but placed it carefully in the blue bin in the truck bed; you never knew these days what you'd need tomorrow. Though he couldn't quite figure what he might need a crushed soda can for, making the world worse than it already was wasn't his first choice.

Thinking of needs, he wouldn't mind a bit of conversation and a welcomed warm body in his bed. He shook his head and shouldered a corpse.

He turned and saw the three men. Two had their rifles, casual, on their shoulders, but one, the stupid-looking one of course, had it aimed.

He heaved the last body onto the pyre. They just watched. His own rifle was in the truck, feet away. Not that it mattered against three.

"Coke's cold," he offered as he removed his Dallas Stars cap and wiped his forehead, all the while watching Stupid with the rifle.

"Lower that, ya redneck idiot," the big hairy one ordered, his laugh definitely forced around the edges. Stupid listened, begrudgingly.

"You're long way from home, Tex," Big said as he presented his hand. A handshake would force him to step farther away from his rifle.

Now I make out if they're actually friendly or just aching to kill. The shake might tell me, but the eyes are a better bet. Neither did.

"I think them Stars might've had half a chance at the cup this year," Big considered in a way that made it clear he wasn't talking hockey.

"Fairies dancing 'round on ice." Stupid bulldozed over the underlying tension. "That ain't no mind skill. Now football, that's like chess —"

"You didn't clean this place just for yourself, did ya?" Big, ignoring Stupid, asked.

"Yep," he replied, knowing they'd think him lying. "Not halfway through the bodies, but I started with the hotel." He hoped they missed mattresses. Then he upped the ante: "Got a stove working."

The quiet one, the one he was damn sure was the leader, spit and spoke. "Hot food and a soft bed is a fine offer for strangers, thank you."

He turned, expecting them to follow, and picked up his rifle from the truck bed. He heard no bolt slide in response, so he continued round the back of the general store.

"You got marshmallows?" Stupid asked.

Marshmallows?

"For the bonfire?"

He chanced a look back at them; they — stone cold detached — kept pace. To see all the dead, all piled there, was more than a horrifying sight, but obviously not to them.

He was in trouble, the dying kind.

He was going to have to add them to the pile.

Killing was easier imagined than done. In fact, except for some angel-of-mercy deals, he'd never actually killed a person or an animal. No matter that they eventually figured out the Infected never healed. No matter that the dying didn't always want to go in a painful puddle of puke and piss. Euthanasia, self-defense: it was all still murder. Maybe he didn't like where this life had dragged him, killing and screaming, but he'd do it.

He turned the corner onto Main Street. They'd parked dirt-crusted motorcycles by the hotel, so staying, at least overnight, was a foregone conclusion.

He glanced over at the general store and was happy to see they hadn't smashed the remaining windows.

"We aren't looters," Big said.

"Am tired of canned shit, wouldn't mind some fresh meat, in more than one way, if you get my drift, hey, Tex?" Stupid liked to blurt agenda.

"I never was much of a hunter and couldn't bring myself to kill if I caught anyway," he answered as dubious looks passed between the three.

The motorcycles were well ridden, and he momentarily thought he was wrong about their intent to stay, but then he saw that the hotel door was ajar.

"Saw you loading the truck, couldn't figure what you was doing, so we looked about a bit before we came to how-do-you-do," Big offered.

Who was the stupid one now? Overly secure in his remote location, he'd been blasting the truck stereo and hadn't even heard the motorcycles, and now they'd pretty much cornered him.

"The town is on a well, so there's showers. Cold, but still," he offered as he crossed the three-story hotel's old-fashioned veranda.

The lobby was shuttered against the heat, and the gloom did little to illuminate the velvet and wood decor he'd so painstakingly restored.

They'd dumped their gear here and chose to carry only rifles to meet and assess him. But it wasn't much, so maybe there were only three of them.

"Kitchen's through there. You'll find food. Stove works, like I said," he said.

"Don't seem like you live here regular," Big stated, rather than asked.

"Yeah, you running a bed and bang, Tex?" Stupid actually clapped him on the shoulder.

The temperature of the dull air dropped degrees.

Stupid removed his hand.

"Stop crowding the man," Leader ordered. "He's solicitous, not accustomed to the company of fools. A personal choice, am I right?"

"Sometimes I don't understand nothing that comes outta your mouth," Stupid whined. And, in that breath, Leader backhanded him to his knees. Instantly, Stupid began to blubber and grovel.

Big stepped back to avoid eye contact and association.

Leader caressed the blade in his belt.

Don't react — but — if they start killing each other, they aren't going to stop there. So, compounding his idiocy and assuring doom, he opened his big mouth. "Just oiled the floors," he drawled.

Leader tensed his shoulders, clenched the hilt of his

blade, but then he cackled like an actual madwoman. "You got yourself a bonfire to light, Tex. Take the bitch out of my sight, and put him to work," Leader ordered. "Otherwise he's worthless."

Big and Stupid looked confused by, and then wary of, this suggested separation. Not that he was pleased with being ordered around either. They hadn't asked his name, hadn't offered theirs; a sign of disassociation, or so said his useless university psych class, but now he was walking away —

He sensed the knife seconds before it would have severed his spine.

He dived onto his hands and kicked Stupid in the gut as the blade sliced his leg.

Rolling to his feet, he saw that Leader was on the veranda, casually lighting a cigar.

Stupid, who'd lost his knife with his fall, charged.

Jesus, he thought as Stupid slammed a shoulder into his rib cage, *it's a goddamned game.*

As proof, Stupid grunted, "Only room for three!"

As he struggled with Stupid, warm blood flooded his leg. *Damn it! Did he slash an artery? Could someone bleed to death from a calf wound?* Then he remembered, he'd never had any damn idea what a damn artery looked like, let alone where the bloody Christ one was in the body.

Stupid, without his knife, wasn't up for twelve rounds. He was mean, but skinny and a little slow. A piece of siding to the head took him down. Winded and light-headed from blood loss, he stared down at the board in his hand. *Damn, now I'm going to have to reboard that window.* Stupid groaned and rolled over on his back.

"To the death, Tex," Leader said cheerfully. "You want his place, you kill him for it."

"Not interested in your sick game," he spat. He probably shouldn't have sneered while saying so, because Leader had that psychotic glint again.

"Allow me to make it perfectly clear: it's you or him," Leader said. Stupid started to cry, not blubbering like before, but silent shaking.

He tossed the piece of siding away. He figured that was a good enough answer.

Leader raised and cocked his rifle. "You going to die for a man who would have willingly killed you? We are the chosen ones in this revitalized, reborn world, but here a man has to step up, has to fight for his existence. Fight or die."

Christ, he's one of those, those messiah complexes.

"Listen, the world that left us behind wasn't half bad," he said. "Why ruin the —"

"Kill him, or I will. He's worthless to me now. Why sacrifice yourself if he's going to die anyway?" Leader argued. "Prove yourself and live."

"Boss, maybe..." Big began to beg, but faltered as Leader turned dead eyes on him. Stupid still silently wept; tears eroded his aggression.

He couldn't stand by and watch a man be killed. Being stupid wasn't an executionable offense.

"None of us survived because we fought some war. We all lucked out. Now, it's a big, empty world, so you go play your game somewhere else." He was insane, gambling with his life, but words continued to flow from his freed mouth. "You're no second coming. You. Just. Lucked. Out."

Leader, his lips stretched across his teeth, aimed. No way to miss this close, so he waited for the bullet to carve through his skull. He heard the shot before he ever felt it, *which was wrong, wrong sense order, wasn't it?* Though maybe a brain had no feeling nerves.

Leader slumped away from the gun that Big still held to his temple. Stupid scrambled to his feet to supplicate himself around Big's knees.

"I ... I ..." Stupid stuttered, his words stopped up with emotion.

"I know, I know, you're welcome. Now you go on ahead, move the body before it stains Tex's patio," Big cajoled. "You won't mind the extra on your pile o' bodies, will ya, Tex?" Big grinned. "You got a nice place here, but we'll be moving on tonight."

Still struck dumb, he watched Stupid haul the body back towards the bonfire. "It's safer ... safer to ... to travel at night," he finally said.

"Yup," Big agreed as he crossed toward the motorcycles. Straddling one, he turned to say, "They don't make 'em like you anymore, Tex."

"My name is Will," he offered.

"Well, Will, thanks for the morality lesson. We won't be seeing you again." Big drowned out his own laugh with the roar of his motorcycle.

He watched until he couldn't catch a glimpse of them on the horizon; then he scrubbed the blood off the veranda while the pyre burned.

SHE'D FOUND A WHEELBARROW FOR THE DOG from one of those urban garden centers. The place seemed stripped of anything remotely food related. A motorcycle with a sidecar, even if she could drive one, would be too conspicuous. Her last group had figured that out the hard way.

The dog's leg was dislocated. She certainly wasn't a vet, but she could read. Finding medical books was as simple as opening the front door of an animal hospital. Stitching through actual flesh was gut wrenching. And still, even calculating for weight, she'd worried about the painkiller and antibiotic dosage.

She'd also found a tiny strawberry plant under the plastic mulch she'd salvaged as rain protection. Wasting precious time, she'd repotted it.

She was headed to the haven of the mountains. They had no reason to follow, except revenge, which, she hoped, wasn't worth it.

Then she saw the sign: REWARD FOR LIVE CAPTURE. The words, a childlike scrawl in red paint, slashed across a billboard from her last modeling gig. The campaign itself was so recent she hadn't cashed the cheque before the dying started. She'd never thought her eyes looked that blue in real life, but they sure did when her face was hawking mascara. *So ... they'd recognized her.*

She glanced down at her chipped fingernails. She was sure she didn't resemble her last film; she'd spent the entire time in a wedding dress and wielding a gun. She wondered what the reward would be; valuables held no value now. This wasn't the first time her face — and body — had gotten her in trouble. Even he had told her — he, her step-father — that he only touched her because she was so beautiful. She was a prize, or a pricey piece of meat.

Rhiannon named the dog B.B. because the Rottie was just blood and bones when she found, rescued, and patched her up. B.B. didn't mind the wheelbarrow.

They traveled evenings to early morning and got off the highway ASAP. When you had no idea where you were going, time didn't factor at all.

She hoped they'd assume she was heading down the coast to LA, but she hadn't been there when the chaos really hit and wasn't ever going back. She placed that life firmly behind her with every step she took.

B.B. didn't stay in the wheelbarrow for more than a few days, which was good, because despite all the Pilates, Rhiannon's shoulders screamed.

Going was slow with B.B. limping. They stopped often for supplies, but never slept where they scavenged. Dog food was oddly easy to find. She tried to not let B.B. gorge, but it was difficult rationing a starving animal, and despite her injury, B.B. bulked up fast.

It was four days before they saw another human.

Memory was a trap as sure as chain or concrete; one that she'd armored against even before she found herself living in a postapocalyptic wasteland, where haunting and terror were everyday events. It didn't do to dwell, wasn't a functional way for her at least, but some days, like today, with the sun warm on her back and B.B.'s nails click, click, clicking on the pavement, her mind wandered.

Often, when people got hint of the bits of terrible she'd confronted in her life, they wondered at the fact that she wasn't lying in a basement somewhere with a needle in her arm and a hole in her soul.

Rhiannon couldn't answer those survivor questions, couldn't be a life coach or some sort of role model, because she had no idea what made her different, what made her brain different than others who had suffered. She had made the best of the situation, controlled it as much as possible, and walked away when she got the chance. Though some ties proved harder to break than others.

Sometimes the other person refused to let go.

In moments of weakness, she worried that the armor — all the years of protective layers built up around her heart and soul — had nothing underneath to protect.

Enough dwelling, Rhiannon. Keep on moving onward. She had a plan — get away — and someone to protect — B.B. — that was as far as she needed to focus.

Except, except... the billboard haunted her. She had thought — when she had time to even think — that she could shed that image and become ... what, she didn't know, but something other than herself. But that billboard, the fact they hadn't raped her, the fact they'd given her a guided tour on the way in. It felt ... *planned? Contrived?* Maybe she was just paranoid after so many years of so many fan stalkers, only one of which had ever laid violent hands on her, and she had to admit, if only to herself, that she had some culpability in that situation.

B.B. pressed a shoulder against her knee, and even before her brain cleared of its memory fog, Rhiannon could feel the tension rippling through the dog's flank.

B.B. must have sensed the man about a mile before, because her nose was glued to the ground.

She, confident they'd left the city behind, had carelessly pushed their traveling farther into daylight.

He, the man, had laid traps.

B.B.'s questing nose dislodged a pile of ripped-up, wilted wildflowers, and Rhiannon yanked the dog backwards seconds from triggering a wicked leghold trap. A trap big enough for a bear.

She froze, standing in the middle of the road with her fist clenched around B.B.'s collar. Every muscle in her body screamed exposure. Sheer rock rose to her left and dropped into a massive river to her right. *No one was crazy enough to ride those rapids. Not anymore.*

She tamped down on her flight instinct. She let her gaze wander farther up the road where seemingly random piles of leaves, weeds, and grass barely covered more traps. So he was a moron, then, but obviously violent.

Whistling.

B.B. growled, her target uncertain but her belly low. Rhiannon finally unfroze and had sense enough to drop to the ground and crawl to the cliff edge. B.B. followed.

He was a hundred feet below: naked, hairy and fishing. *Weren't two of those three illegal?* Or at least they used to be. She'd be worried about that hook, as a man.

The idea of fresh salmon beckoned, but leg traps? *That's a big no way, no how.*

She tried to ease back, but then just as she thought she was out of sight, she dislodged some rock — *shale*, her useless brain offered — with a twist of her foot. In the endless second it took for rock to hit river rock, she wondered if she should put more stock in astrology and that doomsday horoscope she'd read before this bad run.

He saw her.

He shouted.

She ran.

She ran forward, not back, because she was miles past any decent place to hide. B.B. could barely keep up and wouldn't be able to maintain this pace for long.

She twisted her ankle, fell, and bloodied her palms. B.B. whined through her panting.

She looked up to find her forehead inches from a trap.

Fucking bastard. Fuck, fuck, fucking bastard with his little shriveled dick. She didn't give a shit if that river was fed by a glacier or what.

This wasn't the time to fall and stay down. That time

had passed, years before this shit. If her mother hadn't destroyed her, nothing would.

So she got up.

Only then did she see the path carved in the cliff. Unless he had a fucking elevator, they'd be gone long before he got here.

He came for them that night, reeking of rotting fish and human waste. He hadn't bothered to dress; perhaps clothing would have slowed down the plan that was evident by his engorged dick. It was, she noticed, as puny as she'd thought it would be.

He slunk in by the light of her embers, his belly low as he, crawling on all fours, stalked her. She'd expected him, but was still thrown by the sudden, full-body, vicious attack.

Of course, not as thrown as he was by the bear trap in her sleeping bag.

He screamed and thrashed, but still managed to show surprise when she swung down from the tree. Unbelievably, lust hardened his face even more than the pain. She didn't take this as a compliment, knowing that any woman or maybe any warm body would do for this crazy. He considered himself a hunter, after all.

She was sorry to see that the sleeping bag softened the teeth of the trap. Unless it got infected, he probably wouldn't lose the leg. *What a pity.*

"Get this the hell off me!" he demanded. "I wasn't

coming to kill you! I haven't seen a ... woman ... talk ... I just wanted to hear your voice."

"I believe the common way a living being is forced to get out of this sort of mess is to chew their own leg off," she sneered. "Try that."

"Fucking bitch!"

B.B. lunged for his throat, and Rhiannon halfheartedly held her off. Revoltingly, he fear-pissed; the spray soiled her runners.

"You're right about the bitch part, on two counts, but certainly not the fucking." And, leaving him to his hopefully dire fate, she pulled the still snapping and snarling B.B. away.

She always did like a great exit line, though she mourned the loss of a perfectly good sleeping bag.

4 / WILL

THE CRINKLE OF WRAPPERS DREW HIS ATTENTION. He guessed she was about nine, huddled in an aisle at the Drug Mart and inhaling chocolate bars. The absolute terror in her eyes made his stomach knot. This was what the world had become: a girl, mortally terrified, when she saw any man. He couldn't think what the hell to say or do that wouldn't be a threat. *Keep holding the rifle or put it down? Are you alone? Are you okay?*

He was pretty sure that was blood caked underneath her ragged fingernails.

He finally settled for, "Hey, sorry to sneak up on you. I was just gathering some supplies. I live the next town over. My name is Will."

She didn't answer, but her grip on the Snickers bar eased. He continued, "Don't mind me. I'm just going to pick up some shampoo and stuff."

He eased back and crossed into the next aisle to stare at the still-stocked shelves. He didn't need shampoo, but he added it to his box anyway. He could hear her gathering chocolate bars into the sack she wore slung across her shoulders, then silence. He sidestepped to the soap.

Aware of her tracking him, he slowly moved around the store. He fought the urge to grab, feed, and scrub her clean of the blood and bruises.

He briefly contemplated the barrettes, and after he turned the corner, he heard plastic torn and wondered if she had picked the pink ones. He was amazed she'd survived alone all these months, and then realized she probably hadn't been on her own all this time. *Was this her home? Were her parents and siblings now stinking, bloated corpses in a nearby house? Did she still return to them at night? Who'd been feeding her? Or what had happened to her caretakers to force them to abandon her here? Or, even more sickeningly, whose clutches had she escaped?*

He didn't think he was up for this. There had been a few children in the survivor groups he drifted through, but he hadn't taken any responsibility.

He paused in the magazine section and, briefly, wondered if the actress on the *Vanity Fair* cover still had eyes that blue even in death.

The girl's eyes were dark like her matted hair. Will felt like a pedophile as he placed a coloring book and crayons in his now-full box.

She was waiting for him by the entrance, and he briefly wondered how she had gotten in when he'd struggled to prop open the automatic door. He smiled, and she didn't return the gesture. She was clutching another Snickers bar and heavily weighing her options, trying to figure him.

"That's my truck." He gestured with the box toward his Ford, then stepped by her to load the box and the other supplies in the back.

He closed the tailgate just as he heard the passenger

door slam. She buckled up, then sat, clutching her sack and staring straight ahead. He thought he might vomit. He wasn't sure if it was the fear of hurting her further or the trust she'd so readily placed in him that made him ill.

He ripped open a box of granola bars and climbed into the truck. He placed the bars on the seat beside him and shifted the truck into gear.

"Might be stale," he warned; then he ate one anyway.

She reached a tentative hand, caked in dirt and blood, to press play on the stereo. He'd been listening to this on the drive over, but now, the third verse of Paul Simon's "You Can Call Me Al" hit him in the gut. He finally got it. He clenched his jaw to quell the rising emotion. The girl bobbed her head along with the bass line. He'd never had an epiphany before.

In this moment, he chose to become the man he'd always wanted his father to be.

It took one day and three Snickers bars to coax the girl out of the truck, then four more days to convince her that an upstairs bedroom was just as safe as the front hall closet. Will wasn't too sure when she began, finally, to sleep a full night in the bed, but he didn't manage to get her in the bath until he remembered he'd found some animal soaps in the grocery. He'd also offered her a choice between *Star Wars* and Barbie sheets. She picked *Star Wars*, and he wondered if she'd ever seen the movies.

He really didn't know what he was doing. The people who'd built this home hadn't exactly left self-help child-rearing books lying around, but he figured she would need to feel safe alone before she would allow him to be her protector. So to that end, he put together a backpack under her watchful eye.

Will, pleased that he had collected extras, carefully placed all the survival supplies he had on hand on the old farm-style kitchen table. A mini first aid kit, solar blanket, batteryless flashlight, waterproof matches, water packs, and granola bars.

He talked about each item in terms of function and safety as he tucked it away in the backpack. She watched his hands more than his face, but as he zipped the pack and crossed around the table to hand it to her, she slipped off her stool and turned her back so he could slip it over her too-slim-for-such-a-burden arms. She patted his knee and later added her crayons and coloring book to the empty outside pocket.

Then he taught her how to shoot a gun.

OTHER THAN EVIDENCE OF TRAVELERS ALONG THE road, she hadn't seen anyone since Wee Wee a week back, after which she'd changed course twice.

Rhiannon had known something was up the second she entered this middle-of-nowhere town. Except for a few boarded windows, the buildings were ... tidy. Even though the place looked deserted, she leashed B.B. The mountains loomed immediately behind them, but here the land was flat and dry.

After she'd found the Beretta, she traveled by day. It was easier to shoot what you could see, and thanks to lots of film prep, she was deadly.

She eyed the almost inviting hotel, but as she approached the general store, she heard the music. *Paul Simon*, she thought. *He's old, then.*

She adjusted her hat so it was low, but without compromising her sight lines. She'd been dressing as manly as possible for her slight frame.

As if he'd heard her approach, he stepped around the

corner of the store. His rifle was slung over his shoulder. He stopped when he saw them.

B.B. didn't growl.

He grinned, and she was surprised that she noticed he was oddly beautiful — rough, tanned and manly — not her usual type. He threw his head back and laughed, delighted, and then hunkered back on his heels and held his hand out to B.B. She let B.B. off the leash.

B.B. hesitated. The guy wiggled his fingers, still grinning, and to Rhiannon's surprise, B.B. wagged the tail she barely had and bounded to him. B.B. nuzzled his hand. Then he let her lick his face, all the while laughing like a kid. She was unjustifiably jealous of B.B.'s affection.

She moved closer and caught the dark look that passed across his face when he saw B.B.'s numerous newly healed wounds. Then he looked up.

He wasn't old. Maybe younger than her, if she ever admitted her true age. Then, with a thrill, she realized, there was no reason not to.

"It's been months since I've seen a dog," he said.

Now that she was near, she thought he might be part native, but that didn't fit her impression of the twang in his accent. *A native cowboy?* She shouldn't tease, but she thought it best to know quickly how easily he rattled. So she pulled off her glasses and asked, "And a woman?"

HER SKY-BLUE EYES CUT HIS SOUL, THOUGH HE instantly felt stupid for thinking so. He also thought he might know her, but dismissed that.

"About the same," he drawled, glad, not for the first time, that his sister's tendency to leap around corners had made him hard to surprise.

He glanced at the gun on her hip, the knife strapped to her leg, as he slowly gained his feet. He didn't want to stare, but couldn't help it. She'd looked away to survey Main Street, so he could really only see the line of her jaw. She must be sweltering under all those layers.

"Where are all the bodies?" she asked, and he noted that she had no distinguishable accent.

"I cleaned," he replied, blunt but kind about it.

"Ah," she breathed, and then actually raised her perfect nose to sniff the air. "Bonfire," she concluded.

"Seemed best," he agreed.

She stepped away to look into the store. He'd been restocking the shelves, which, he was aware, might make him seem more than a little crazy.

"You alone?" He called her attention back, but then instantly regretted the tension his aggression evoked as she placed her hand on her gun.

"Just B.B. and me," she answered testily. The dog glanced at the woman, opened its mouth in a big grin and lifted its nose for another pat.

"Well, I imagine you're both hungry," he offered, and was confused when her jaw clenched and she looked out of town as if planning to leave.

"Just because you didn't rape me at first sight doesn't mean I'm your friend," she finally sneered, and he caught the edge of fear in her.

"I never did make friends easy." He spoke in a light tone like he would with a wounded animal, which, he didn't have to guess, she'd been. The woman looked at the dog, B.B., who hadn't left his side, and then suddenly, he could feel the utter weariness she didn't let show.

She pulled a glove off and offered him her gun hand. "Rhiannon," she said. Her skin seared his when he folded his callused hand around hers.

He held her eyes with his own, which were dark brown, and then, with a grin, offered his name. "Will." She remembered she should let go of his hand.

He sauntered around the store, with B.B. at his heels. She knew she would follow, but momentarily thought of the freedom she had found alone. He looked back, not assuming her compliance, but really genuine in his concern, which was almost impossible to fake even for the most cunningly skilled.

B.B. trusts him, her weary brain offered while her gut screamed to keep on moving and moving on. She was just too tired to keep walking.

B.B. climbed into the back of the truck like she did it every day. Maybe she had; her history was a mystery, not like her own puppet strings. The truck was an old red Ford, and Rhiannon wondered if he liked pretending to be a cliche; a certain safety came with playing a role. He opened the door for her, but then crossed to the driver's side.

"You have gasoline," she stated.

"No one to compete with," he replied.

She climbed in and immediately started digging through the glove box. He didn't seem to mind; she found a handgun, a knife, and granola bars.

"Perhaps it's rude to mention, but the two of you look more than a little banged up, though mostly healed, so..." He let the question linger.

"I took care of it," she answered tersely. True, that bill-board still haunted her, but there was no way they'd be following her through all her random turns.

"I'm sorry it was necessary at all —" he started, but she cut him off.

"That's just the world we live in now."

He didn't push the subject.

They continued in silence for another ten minutes. Then, the road rapidly left the little town behind and curved into the mountain valley. Seemingly at random, Will stopped and hopped out of the truck to clear some brush, drove in, and then concealed the entrance to the turn-off again. So he left the town open and inviting, but hid where he laid his head. She wondered what that said about him, but was really not into analyzing anything at the moment.

A large well-kept house was nestled in the evergreens at the end of a long driveway. Its cedar shingles had grayed. Will parked by the front double doors.

Still not sure about this, Rhiannon crossed to the truck bed and lowered the tailgate to put B.B. on the leash. Will grabbed a box of supplies, which included Froot Loops cereal: odd choice for a grown man.

She turned to the house and saw a nine-year-old girl holding a sawed-off shotgun trained on her. The girl held the gun hip high and wedged against a front patio post.

"Ahh." Actually, she didn't know what to say. Will carted his box up the stairs, and the girl adjusted her aim around him as he passed.

"This is Snickers," Will said as he entered the house.

The girl didn't move, so Rhiannon didn't move.

B.B. also seemed a little unsure.

Will crossed back out.

"Um, she's your sister?" she asked as he grabbed another box from the truck.

"Nope," he unhelpfully responded.

"Hello, Snickers," she tried.

No response.

"Snickers doesn't talk much, like, not once since we met, but she's a great cook!" Will said.

"And, I'm guessing, she can shoot that gun," she said grimly.

"Wouldn't do her much good if she couldn't," he replied. "We practice, lots. Snickers, that's enough aiming of the gun. This is B.B. and Rhiannon. I wouldn't bring them here if I thought they'd hurt you."

Snickers grudgingly lowered the shotgun, slung it across her shoulders with a silk scarf she had tied to each end, and entered the house.

So we're not his first strays, Rhiannon thought, and instantly felt more at ease. The girl looked unscathed, definitely loopy, but no bruises. And, even though she knew it was a dangerous thought to have in this chaotic reality, she actually whispered out loud, "Maybe, maybe this is all going to be okay."

Then she followed B.B., who was already loping off into the house.

He'd been worried about the introduction, had hoped the presence of the dog would smooth it, but B.B. didn't seem to register for Snickers. He felt off. Snickers's shotgun swung from her shoulders, Rhiannon all but radiated heat behind him, and B.B.'s nails clicked on the hardwood.

They'd settled into a kind of routine, Snickers and him, for the last ten days, but Rhiannon was an unknown, another in a long list.

Snickers climbed on her stool to stir the pasta sauce she had made. He put the box on the table and turned to catch Rhiannon's reaction. Rhiannon stared at the working electric stove and raised her hand to flick the light switch. The light over the kitchen table turned on.

"Electricity?" she asked.

"Multiple generators," he answered, trying to stop his chest from swelling too large, but enjoying her amazement.

Snickers crossed to turn off the light and then resumed chopping carrots.

"We're still careful about how much we use," he said.

"Fresh veggies?" Rhiannon moaned as she removed her hat to expose her golden hair. He could feel the silly grin taking over his face again.

"Greenhouse out back, self-watering. It was crazy overgrown, but Snickers has tamed it." He was happy he sounded steady, despite the grin.

Rhiannon swayed, dead on her feet. He reached for her despite the wary look Snickers threw his way, but she stepped out of his grasp.

"You'll want a shower," he offered as cover. "The bedroom to the left of the main bath has clothes that might fit." He indicated the stairs.

Rhiannon looked unsure, but seemed compelled to ask, "A hot shower?"

"You wouldn't want a cold one," he teased.

"Right." She seemed to be lost within her own thoughts.

"Snickers, we'll have to pick up dog food for B.B.," he said. Snickers leaped down to write DOG FOOD on the magnetic list on the fridge.

Rhiannon looked like her head might implode, and Will worried he was playing it too cool. If B.B.'s appearance was any indication, they'd been through hell and more.

"Or you could sleep," he started, but then Rhiannon snapped to awareness.

"Yes, thank you ... I ... thank you." She backed out of the room with B.B.

Will stepped forward to watch Rhiannon climb the stairs.

Snickers tossed carrots into the sauce.

He placed a hand on her tiny head, a gesture she accepted now.

"Maybe she'll stay, maybe not," he soothed, "but we'll be okay either way. I found some Wagon Wheels." He pulled the peace offering from the box of supplies.

THE CLOTHES DIDN'T FIT, BUT SHE DIDN'T CARE. They were clean and actually pretty ... well, compared to the black canvas she'd been swathed in. The shower had been hot, just like he, Will, had said. There was honey and vanilla in the soap, and Rhiannon had almost started crying at the smell.

When she'd stepped out of the shower to make sure the door was locked for the second time, she noticed that B.B. was asleep on the floor. *B.B. feels safe*, she scolded herself, but then chafed at the idea of a man protecting her. *What if, what if*, her brain clamored, but never completed.

She'd heard him calling when she was dressing, but still testing him, she didn't answer. He passed her open door on the way to the bathroom.

"Rhiannon? Dinner," he called.

"Yeah?" she murmured. He turned back, and she, wearing only a skirt, made sure her bare back faced the door. She knew he'd caught sight. All the air sucked from the room. She pulled her shirt on, noting in the mirror that he stared steadily away.

"You up for some dinner? We found some canned meat for B.B." His voice broke slightly, but maybe only a trained ear would have caught it.

"Thanks. We'll be right there." She turned toward him, but he didn't look at her as he left. She felt oddly aroused, or maybe disappointed, but definitely awake.

Later, after the dishwashing — he'd dried — Rhiannon sat in the living room bay window and watched the sunset burn the sky behind the mountains.

B.B. slept by the unlit fireplace.

Will read a book, *World War Z* of all choices.

Rhiannon breathed. She hadn't been this calm in... maybe ever. She watched Snickers, who was crashed on the sofa and cuddled up with her shotgun. She felt the moment Will's attention hit her.

"We're locked in for the night if that's what's worrying you," he whispered.

She shook her head and indicated the gun. "Not loaded, is it?"

"Wouldn't do her much good if it wasn't," he replied, and returned to his book.

"That your answer for everything?" she asked.

He laughed and then soberly stated, "It's a world gone mad."

Quickly changing the subject, she tried, "How long have you guys been here?"

He shrugged and guessed. "Two months, maybe, for me. Ten days for Snickers."

"Snickers?" she asked.

"Were what she was eating," he answered.

"Amazing she didn't get snatched. If it's not the rebuild humanity one-rape-at-a-time group, it's murderers or the Infected."

"The Infected?" he asked, and she was glad she had recent news to offer for his generosity. She never did like owing anyone.

"They figured out how to stave off death."

"What?" He couldn't get his jaw up. "Jesus. Not a cure, though?"

"No," she replied. "But the blood of the immune can sustain them indefinitely."

He was reeling, working it out. "But the virus burns through the body's resources, like consuming the Infected from the inside out."

"Large doses of blood," she added. "It sustains them, but the virus symptoms are still present, so they're sick, but fast, strong, angry —"

"And in need of our blood," Will whispered. He glanced at Snickers, who was now sucking her thumb. "Living, breathing monsters. Nice."

"Rebuild Humanity keeps them as pets," she added casually. Nevertheless, she could feel the questions he didn't ask practically burning her.

He settled on, "You lost someone?"

"With 99.9 percent of the worldwide population wiped out, we all lost," Rhiannon countered, but Will just shrugged. Then there'd been no one special for him, before. She could say the same and they could bond over never truly being loved, but she didn't.

That night, the terrors started. Rhiannon was trapped in utter darkness with one of them, the Infected, its putrid snot dripping on her face right before it —

She woke, hoping she hadn't screamed.

H E THOUGHT HE HEARD R HIANNON SCREAM, BUT as he continued to try to sense her through the multiple walls that separated them, Will got nothing. He'd been awake all night, his brain too full to turn off, not a problem he ever had in the past. He'd watched her, collecting clues: *perfect table manners ... hesitation with the dishwashing ...* She wasn't used to this life. Again, it had nagged him, that feeling that he knew her. He wondered if she was going to stay. He wondered if it came to it, whether or not he'd ask her to. *For himself? Or Snickers?*

He was pretty sure Snickers should be talking by now. He was starting to think maybe she was mute; maybe he shouldn't have given her the gun, but he couldn't start second-guessing, not even with Rhiannon's doubt. He thought of the Fleetwood Mac song and wondered if he could still play it. Not that he'd picked up a guitar since college.

Movement at the door distracted him, and he turned his head, expecting Snickers but, traitorously, hoping for

Rhiannon. It was Snickers, sans gun. He patted the bed beside him and she, dragging all her bedding, climbed up. *Maybe one of her parents might have been part Asian?*

Now, with Snickers awake, he was pretty sure Rhiannon must have screamed, because it'd been days since the child had needed to crawl in with him.

Snickers stared at him with her almond-shaped cat eyes, and as he always did, not knowing what she needed, he just let her look. She raised her hand to suck on her thumb and he pulled it away gently with a smirk. She smiled at this, their habitual, familiar behavior.

He heard more movement at the door as Rhiannon and B.B. silently slipped in. They curled into bed with Snickers wedged in the middle.

Snickers curled her hand in the hair at the side of Will's neck, and he realized how long it was getting. B.B. sighed as only a satisfied dog can.

He was glad he'd claimed the master bedroom with its king-sized bed. The responsibility had scared him at first, but now Rhiannon was here. Smiling as he closed his eyes to finally sleep, he thought maybe he could see the first glimmer of dawn at the edges of the blinds.

He later thought it was the worst damn idea he'd ever had, and he'd done many stupid things. Taking the girls with him, beyond stupidity.

A road trip, he'd suggested. The girls glowed with excitement, and he'd felt so damn satisfied. Only four hours south, they'd be back before dark.

He'd been systematically collecting supplies from the surrounding towns, to restock the store, hotel, and houses. He didn't know why.

He hadn't ventured this far since he acquired Snickers, but he thought it would be fun and get Rhiannon out for the first time in weeks.

They'd relaxed into a rhythm, but he had noticed the strawberry plant in her bedroom. Even with room in the garden, she hadn't planted it.

Rhiannon saw the gun shop as soon as they entered town, and in minutes, the bullet belt was around Snickers's waist. So the gun idea was okay now. Will attempted to be pleased rather than smug.

Rhiannon went clothes hunting. Snickers stuck with him. He hoped to add rarities to the hotel library, but prioritized medical supplies.

He left Snickers by the magazines, she liked the pictures, and went to box as much antibiotics, painkillers, and whatever else he could carry.

He hadn't realized that B.B. was with him until she started to growl a deep warning just as his hand reached for the box of condoms.

"Hey, it's not like that." He started to back away. Then he saw the hulking shadow by the window. *Jesus H. Christ, what the hell was that?*

B.B. couldn't get lower to the ground and still move, and she was scaring the hell out of him with her noises. He set his box down.

He suddenly had a terrible feeling he was about to come face to face with Rhiannon's and B.B.'s past.

SHE DIDN'T KNOW AT THE TIME WHAT THE FUCK she'd ever do with the grenades, or how the hell they got into the gun shop in the first place, but she took them anyway. She also scored a cool MEC backpack. She remembered her hair had almost been that orange, same as the pack, in her first starring role — kicking vampire ass with great dialogue — still one of her favorites. The side pocket was perfect for grenades, and the water bottle holder adapted nicely to a shotgun. She took as much ammo as she could carry.

The bullet belt was too big for Snickers, but Rhiannon punched another hole with her Swiss Army knife. She'd always had to be easily adaptable.

Currently, she was appalled at the plethora of pink in the girls clothing section; maybe Snickers would prefer boys' browns and blues? She grabbed and stuffed; she'd never been much of a shopper even when it had been expected, with her millions and all that. She got winter stuff too, in case it got picked over.

It was at that moment she realized she was planning to stay.

Was such domestic happiness even possible? She'd stopped dreaming of such, young, around the time she'd torn the horse photos off her walls. Around the time her childhood had been forcefully, or perhaps sneakily, stolen from her. Around the time she'd learned that no one, no matter their title or blood tie, would step up to protect her, even when she asked for help. She guessed she'd been just a little older than Snickers currently was —

She heard the chains dragging on the concrete sidewalks before she saw them. Asked earlier, she would have thought she'd freeze in fear, but she didn't.

It was him: Shotgun-Fucking-Asshole, though he was missing an ear now. She was going to fucking blow his head off, right through the store window.

Then, like a cold shower, she thought of Snickers. *Had she and Will moved from the drugstore?* Still hidden, Rhiannon spied through the window.

The Ford was still parked by the gun shop. She couldn't see anything through the Drug Mart windows. *Fuck.*

And where the fuck was B.B.?

She left the clothing box by the front door, because she'd fucking be back for it, and then slipped into the back alley.

HE DIDN'T HAVE A LEASH, SO HE TIED A TENSOR bandage around B.B.'s collar. Together, they silently shifted until they had eyes on Snickers.

She seemed to be scrutinizing a *Vanity Fair* cover. Then, coming to some sort of decision, she turned as if to bring him the magazine. She'd only taken a step when she spotted him and B.B. partway down the aisle. Chocolate was smeared across one of her cheeks.

Then the army-jacketed guy grabbed her, twisting her into a football tuck as he ripped the magazine from her little hands.

B.B. didn't even twitch when Will changed his mind about the Tensor leash: all her muscle was homed on her prey.

"Who's this, kid? Who's the pretty on the cover?" Army cajoled. Then he slammed Snickers on his shoulder to knock the breath and fight out of her.

B.B. took him out at the knees before Army saw what hit him.

Will caught Snickers before she hit the linoleum face-first, then still managed to stop Army from bludgeoning B.B. with his gun.

Snickers wasn't happy to be placed to the side, and Will heard her pump the shotgun a split second before she got it in Army's snarling face. He yanked the barrel up and to the side as Snickers pulled the trigger, and the redirected shot took out an entire window with spray.

Army's body slammed into Will's chest and knocked him back. He wrenched the shotgun from Snickers's hands as he fell, and then lost it underneath the shelves.

They wrestled, their footing insecure in the fallen magazines. If not for B.B. clamped to Army's leg, he'd be seriously outmatched. At the edge of his vision, he could see Snickers burrowing under the shelving to retrieve her gun.

Rhiannon burst through the back door like some avenging angel. Her entrance seriously distracted Army. Course, Will felt that way every time he saw her, so it didn't come as a surprise to him.

He grabbed Snickers and rolled as Rhiannon spun to crack the side of Army's skull with the butt of her gun.

Snickers scrambled from his arms to stare down at Army, who was out cold but breathing. B.B.'s lingering snarls summed up Will's own feelings nicely.

"Move, Will," Rhiannon urged as she wrapped her hand around B.B.'s collar and pulled the dog away. "There's no way they'd miss shotgun fire."

"They?" he groaned as he got up and followed Rhiannon out the alley door.

"Two more, and one of — them — the Infected," she warned as she soothingly smoothed Snickers's hair, then gave the child her secondary gun.

"We get to the truck and go," he firmly stated, but

Rhiannon just smiled, almost sweetly. "No, Rhiannon. Not with Snickers here."

That momentarily stalled Rhiannon, but they didn't have time for another plan before they heard footsteps, crunching glass, and loud cursing coming from inside the drugstore.

"Rhiannon," he ordered, "you take Snickers and hide, somewhere with a big, locked door between you and them. I'll lead them out of town."

"Oh, yeah? Hide the useless females?" Rhiannon growled, but he cut her off.

"No. You don't hesitate or compromise. You're the gunslinger here."

She wasn't that easily convinced.

"I need you to do this, Rhiannon. Snickers will be safe with you."

So she scooped Snickers up and was gone.

She left. Just like that. *No goodbye. Christ, get your head in the game! You begged. She did.* So, heart in his throat, Will turned back into the store.

He almost made it to the truck before he saw It: the Infected. It was lumbering up the far sidewalk toward him. It sniffed the air in his direction and then bellowed.

He was happy he hadn't eaten, because despite frozen limbs, he was pretty sure he could and would throw up.

It dragged two broken chains.

Two guys, one missing an ear, sprinted from around the

side of the drugstore after it. They shouted and actually gestured at him to flee.

He did.

Why didn't he just climb in the Ford and drive off? Because he was an absolute, goddamn, going-to-hell idiot.

He ran; It was faster.

It didn't care he used to be an all-star quarterback.

It didn't care track and field had been his yearly charity gig.

It. Wanted. His. Blood.

He didn't know the town footprint. He made a wrong turn, but was actually able to leap the fence that blocked his way. The Infected just tore through.

Then It had him pinned.

He noted, as he was choke-pressed against a brick building that he thought might have been the bank, that It still had a couple of fence boards on its arm.

It bit his shoulder.

He screamed. He couldn't help it.

Then they were there, yanking at its chains. The one-eared guy cursed up a firestorm, but Will couldn't hear him for the pain of being eaten alive.

Seeing the missing ear triggered his deadened brain. He fumbled for his knife, conveniently strapped to his thigh in homage to Rhiannon, and thrust it in the Infected's ear. The blade slid in easier than he'd expected, and the force of the blow dented the side of its head.

It didn't like that, but It did drop him.

"Don't kill it," One Ear yelled, and proved he was insane.

The Infected cat-batted the jutting knife and got it loose along with a chunk of its brain. The mushed brain matter squelched under the knife as it hit the ground. They all, including It, just stared dumbfounded at the goopy pile.

The pain in his shoulder focused Will quicker than the others. He got the chain looped around the Infected's neck seconds before its bloodlust awoke.

It thrashed.

He had to climb onto its back to keep the chain tight, but he soon figured out that cutting off its airway had little effect.

One Ear got its attention with a blood transfusion bag.

His buddy grabbed for the chain.

It slathered the blood.

They got it, minimally, controlled.

Soon as he stepped back, One Ear had a gun to his head.

"Hurting our pal back there was unnecessary. We only have questions."

"Army attacked. I responded." Will grimaced. He glanced at the burning brand that was his shoulder. It wasn't as mangled as it felt.

"Bite won't infect you, doesn't work like that, case you cared," One Ear said, as apologetic as someone could be with a gun to your head.

"Doesn't mean it won't kill me." He made a sympathy play, but there was little to be had.

"Drug Mart looked well stocked. But before you patch yourself up, like I said, we got questions. Answer nice and we won't let our friend here have another taste," One Ear said.

"This piece of real estate we're looking for was sighted heading this way about two weeks ago; she's on foot, with a dog," One Ear's buddy elaborated.

"Haven't seen anyone except you —" He started in

denial, but ended in a scream as One Ear whacked his gun, hard, across his shoulder wound.

He might have blacked out for a bit, because when he came aware, he was on his hands and knees, staring at his bile mixed with the Infected's brains.

"We've been gone way long," One Ear rambled. "I'm real tired of walking 'cause we got to drag It with us, and we're super low on blood packs."

Will really didn't feel like engaging in woe-is-me conversation, so he kept quiet and listened for a way out, but One Ear wasn't forthcoming on that topic.

"Point is, it needs feeding, and excepting your blood immunity, you're no value to us." One Ear finished with an almost friendly toe nudge.

Will didn't doubt the truth of those few words, but he'd never heard his self-worth laid out so precisely and with such doomsaying before. *One man could repopulate the earth with enough fertile women.* He wasn't that man. *Course, in a generation, inbreeding would be a problem.* He continued to keep quiet.

The Infected didn't seem to be doing well without its missing brain chunk. The right side of its face was running down into its neck.

"Shit, this guy don't know," the buddy whined.

"Of the two of you fools, why Hal had to be the one to get his head bashed in," One Ear griped. "He doesn't ask questions, not about us, who we're looking for, or It, means he knows or has heard about the Infected, about us."

"Right." Despite his agreement, Buddy didn't get the drift.

As he hunkered down beside Will, One Ear twirled his gun, once, like his wrist ached.

"You're going to want to bind that bite before you lose

so much blood —" One Ear got his gun grabbed as punishment for his near friendliness. Will twisted One Ear's wrist to the breaking point, got his own finger also over the trigger and the barrel up One Ear's rather wide nostril. One Ear was more angry than scared. It bothered Will that, even with the upper hand, he just pissed people off. At least Buddy freaked out.

The Infected, done with the packed blood, sniffed the air and started pawing the ground in his direction. One Ear smirked. "It takes two of us to hold it."

"How do you know, with me and my bloody wound so near, it won't take a bite of you by mistake? It don't seem to hold its relationships too close."

One Ear looked uneasy at that line of reasoning, and they slowly negotiated a standing position that placed One Ear's back to the Infected and Buddy.

"I'm just passing through, you're just passing through," Will suggested. "We continue on, forget we met, and you two try to not get eaten."

"You don't get it, Cowboy," One Ear nasally explained. "The Boss don't accept no empty hands or, worse, excuses." He indicated his lack of ear.

"Listen," Will countered, getting frustrated, "I think we —"

"They aren't going to listen to your negotiations, Will." Rhiannon, armed and dangerous, stepped into the alley.

The Infected groaned and strained at its neck chain enough that Buddy's feet slipped a bit in the packed dirt.

He felt his blood pressure spike, but not in a good way, at Rhiannon's appearance.

"Hello, dolly! Remember me?" One Ear practically beamed.

"Sure do," Rhiannon answered, and then, leveling her shotgun, blew the Infected's head off.

The close-range blast destroyed what was left of its brain.

It crumpled.

Buddy, shrieking, dropped the now useless chain and pawed at the splatter of brain remnants on his face.

One Ear's mouth hung limp even as his eyes bulged. He shoved the gun away from his nose, and, still staring at It on the ground, let out a keening moan.

In a step, Rhiannon had Buddy knocked down with her foot on his chest.

"Will, have you got the asshole covered or not?" she demanded.

One Ear had fallen to his knees by the Infected and seemed to be having some sort of breakdown. He began wailing and practically foaming at the mouth.

"Jesus, oh, Jesus, oh Jesus," Buddy, completely terrified by One Ear's behavior, blubbered. He didn't get what the hell was going on either.

Even Rhiannon was thrown, and characteristically, she responded with anger. "Fuck, asshole. It was already dead. I did it a fucking favor."

One Ear shut up. He just stopped: wailing, moving, everything. Even the echo of his howls abandoned the alley. Then finally, he turned his red, deadened eyes to Rhiannon. She met his gaze.

"It was my brother," he said. "You killed my brother."

"You chained him — It — made it eat people, prolonged its unnatural and painful existence, and you call yourself brother?" Rhiannon retorted.

"I'll have you, bitch," One Ear snarled. "Own you. Boss

or no Boss, not to kill, no, but you'll beg for a bullet every time I rip you —"

"That's enough!" Will shouted. "You attack? You better expect people to defend! Now, get your asses out of town before I regret letting you."

"Watch it, Cowboy," One Ear sneered, "you'll find there's lots of people willing to kill for her."

"And die, it seems," Rhiannon, rather inappropriately, retorted.

He watched, for what he was aware was the second time, as morally challenged men left town. The difference was he was pretty sure these guys would be back, bigger and stronger. He figured it was better they assumed he and Rhiannon had settled in this place, but there was no way he'd let them lay eyes on Snickers.

They didn't take Army with them, and while he figured that was a good deal for Army, he was aware of what it said about One Ear and his buddy, and how far they'd go to get hands on Rhiannon.

Snickers, seated between them, played with the CDs. The girl had the habit of playing certain songs on repeat. She seemed particularly fond of "Landslide."

The wind tangled Rhiannon's hair until she ponytailed it rather than roll up the window, but still Will didn't speak to her or Snickers.

They'd watched the trackers leave town at gunpoint. They left their army-jacketed friend still out cold in the Drug Mart, and that said something not so nice about them. There was no way Will would've let her take care of them, even if she had suggested it.

In moments like these, she was starting to doubt her humanity.

She'd left Snickers, with B.B. guarding, in the attic of the church. They would've never found her, but Will didn't care about that part. Of course, if he never spoke to her again, she'd never know if he just hated being rescued or being disobeyed. Neither option was cool with her.

She was worried they would track them, but Will was

too smart for that. The drive home ended up taking four hours longer than the drive down.

She'd tended his shoulder before they retrieved Snickers. She knew he didn't want the girl to see his blood or hear the pain of the stitches.

Rhiannon had never had a man just not talk to her before. They were always talking, always wooing, demanding, or even justifying throwing her away.

She refused to say sorry. She had waited awhile. He might have made it out or, worse, been eaten, so she checked and found him having a little chat with the bad guys.

She broke the silence first; she always had been weak that way. "So, are you going to be mad through dinner, because us girls need to eat."

"This is not a conversation I am having in front of Snickers," Will answered.

"She was safe, Will, with B.B. and a secret safety knock!"

Snickers obligingly demonstrated their code knock on the dash.

"She begged me to go," Rhiannon continued. "You think she wants to lose you?"

Will snorted doubtfully, but did cast a sideways glance at Snickers. She met his gaze with what were probably wide eyes full of unexpressed worry mixed with residual terror. She saw the first moment Will began to melt — his emotional barrier wasn't for Snickers — and she instantly decided that she didn't want to use Snickers as a buffer. Didn't want him to forgive her, or at least brush his concerns away out of love for the child.

"I'm sorry I disobeyed you." She laid on the sarcasm. He snorted again.

"You've your own mind, Rhiannon," he gently stated. "And I very much like that, but this isn't about you and me disagreeing on a plan." He was managing her again. It should upset her that she was something to be managed, but she felt he did it for her inner peace, not his.

"I will never put her in harm's way or choose myself or you over her safety to my dying breath," Rhiannon vowed and meant it. Will looked at her then.

"Truth and promise?" he asked.

"Yes." Then she reflected, "I've never placed someone else's life before my own."

"Neither have I," he agreed.

After that, Will didn't speak again, not for a long time. And this time she didn't fight the silence, nor did it haunt her.

As the sky darkened, Snickers tucked sideways between and on them, and slept.

"Chicken or fish for dinner?" he joked, as if life was good and simple, as if they hadn't just almost had to kill or be killed hours before.

Snickers curled her toes right around the finger she had just softly stroked along her foot. Will's adoring grin crinkled around his eyes. She realized then and there she was head over heels, from the bottom of her soul, completely in love with both of them.

She was going to have to leave.

HE KNEW SOMETHING WAS WRONG THE MOMENT he saw the flickering light through the hotel windows; actually, a few houses were also candlelit. With the girls asleep, he had decided to drive through his village to make sure all was well before heading home. All was not well.

He kept the place stocked and was always on the lookout for repairs and such, but why, he wasn't sure. Not visitors, not since Snickers became his priority.

He could have circled, dropped the girls or even come back in the morning, but he didn't. Maybe he should make "stupid" his middle name.

The U-Haul, hitched to the pickup, gave a grinding groan as he slowed the truck and turned off the headlights. They were heavy with supplies. Why the hell did he compulsively stock and supply the damn village? Now his obsession would put the girls in harm's way for the second time today.

Rhiannon's whisper through the dark caused him to violently flinch. "Who do you think they are, Will?"

"Friendlies, I hope," he answered.

"Well, they haven't trashed the place, and you do have that vacancy sign hung."

"For authenticity, not as a welcome," he muttered.

"You could flip it to no vacancy."

Normally he was happy to hear her teasing vocal lilt, but right now he didn't want her laughing at him.

"I'm going to check them out. You'll take Snickers safely home?" That ended up sounding like a question, which he didn't like, but she got it.

"I already promised, Will, but ..."

"If I don't come home, then you'll know ... you'll know to run." He tried to sound matter of fact about it.

Rhiannon climbed over Snickers as he slid out the driver's side.

"No lights," he cautioned. She just nodded while not looking at him.

"Ya know how to drive stick, don't ya, little lady?" he drawled to lighten the mood, and got a smile from Rhiannon for it.

"You'll take B.B."

Unlike his, her statements never sounded like questions. He nodded, and B.B., who had seemingly followed the conversation, leaped off the back of the truck to join him.

She kissed him then, their first kiss. Her hand was hard, almost harsh, against the back of his neck, and their connection quick and fierce. He brushed his rough thumb against her silky cheek and tried to soften the kiss; she yielded, but only for a moment. Then she turned away.

She started the pickup and again refused to look at him, but B.B. got a laugh and a quick nuzzle when she propped herself up on the door.

As Rhiannon carefully backed away, Snickers's head

popped up to look at him through the front window. Her eyes were as hollow as his stomach felt.

B.B., already on alert, stared at the hotel, but he watched until the truck was swallowed in the dark, an image he prayed wasn't foreboding.

He could hear at least three people talking inside, and, as he approached, a rifle-armed shadow rose from its smoke break on the deck chaise. He paused, his foot hovering over the bottom of three steps onto the veranda, and looked up at the shadow.

"Tex?" a man questioned.

As the shadow moved near the candlelight that filtered through the windowed front doors, it became Stupid, grinning, as if he'd won a prize.

"TEX!" Stupid shouted, and, before he could respond, Big flung open the doors to laugh and clap him on the shoulder like you do to a buddy.

"We thought you'd left us. We brought people for you to meet!" Big crowed. "We'd been telling them, ladies especially, about your place. Well, the ladies said we'd like to sleep on mattresses and have running water, so why don't we go visit your friend Tex? I thought, why not, Tex has got all that space and done all that fixing, he must like visitors, nice ones at least, so we came back." Big finally paused to breathe and then looked at him expectantly.

"How many people have you brought here, Big?"

Big beamed at the nickname. "Oh, 'bout fifteen or so... five ladies." Even within the shadows, he could see Big's face grow dark. "We lost two before we turned this way ... poachers." Big must have seen his hesitation, because he quickly added, "Everyone joins us and stays by their own choice, not at gunpoint."

Stupid, who had uncharacteristically been silent,

though grinning, up to this point, contributed, "You got it," to the conversation.

Will suddenly felt he was being pitched, hard and fast, a useless product he never had liked, understood, or wanted in the first place.

"It's a hotel, for stopping by, not staying," he stated firmly.

"Right," Big countered. "But the houses —"

"Not available," he interrupted.

"I told you, I told you he weren't gonna forgive for me trying to kill him," Stupid moaned.

"That ain't it, is it, Tex?" Big asked.

"You're welcome to stay a couple of days while you figure out where you'll head," he offered, though even that was longer than he liked.

"The world's our oyster, hey?" Big eyed him thoroughly, but kept his tone light.

Will nodded, and unexpectedly, found he had to look away.

"You're a hard man, Tex," Big stated, and almost as an afterthought, he added, "You must have something really very precious to protect."

"We're leaving, then, Big?" Stupid tested out the new nickname.

"The road south is clear for about four car hours, at least," Will offered.

"Yeah, you been busy, we seen, Tex. We just hoped ... we're good people, we hoped you'd take us in, maybe lead us, like." Big didn't want to beg.

"You got me mixed up with someone. I'm no leader. Can barely take care of myself." He needed to leave before he got talked into anything. He stepped back off the veranda. "I have some fresh blueberries I'll bring 'round tomorrow morning," he offered as pitiful consolation.

"That's kind of you, Tex, real kind." Big gave him a mini salute. Stupid managed to look actually sorrowful as he lit another cigarette.

He felt their eyes the whole way out of town. Of course, he headed the opposite way and had to double back to get home.

Rhiannon had waited up.

"Was it ... was it about me again?" she asked tentatively from her vantage point on the sofa. She and Snickers both had shotguns at the ready.

"Course not," Will replied evenly. "Just a group. They understand they need to be moving on; wouldn't be surprised if they're gone by morning."

He saw something there, etched in Rhiannon's face. But candlelight didn't provide illumination, and then Snickers raised her arms to him. She'd never asked to be carried to bed before. For a smaller man, she'd be too big for it, but right now he welcomed the distraction.

By morning, he wished he'd taken the time to decipher Rhiannon. But by then it was too late, and he'd lost all his girls.

She'd waited until they all were asleep, including B.B. Actually, she listened to them breathe for a while before she tore herself away.

Then she wrote a note to leave on the kitchen table. She didn't use the word love, but she meant it. She wrote about their safety instead. She thanked them for taking care of her and B.B. She had too much to say and not enough paper; her writing was cramped and messy at the end. She asked Snickers to take care of B.B., mostly because she'd feel better if the dog was always at the girl's side, shotgun or no shotgun.

She also left the strawberry plant, still happy in its bigger pot. She hoped Snickers would plant it and it would provide sweet treats for years.

She thought, momentarily, that she might die from the pain of it, just sitting there, bent over that note, but her death wouldn't protect them. She had to be seen, separate from them, by the relevant parties. She'd worry about getting sighted and then getting away later. It didn't matter where Shotgun Asshole and his buddy were currently, because they had to eventually follow the river to get to the city.

She mapped a direct route rather than the meander she'd taken here, avoiding the village. She didn't need another group recognizing her.

She had asked them not to follow, and Will would accept her decision. Not that he wouldn't disagree or fight; he just picked winnable battles.

She'd thought about making love to him tonight, but was sure he would hate her even more by morning if she could leave after such intimacy. She'd never broken up with anyone. She always played it out to the ruined end. In this case, leaving was a gesture of true love, not hate.

She didn't bother traveling by night, except the first one. The point was to be seen, but by day two, she was worried they'd outpaced her. She should have known that Shotgun Asshole never planned to return empty-handed, but was simply regrouping before selecting his next route. There was only one way, along the edge of the river, out of the mountains. From there, if you kept to the road, you had three routes to choose from.

First time out, they must have taken the low road and wound up four hours south of Will's village. It was just luck, or perhaps fate, that she, Will, and Snickers had been scavenging there that day. The village itself wasn't on any of the three direct routes. She had randomly twisted and turned until she found Will.

This time, without their monster, they wouldn't be on foot, so neither was she. A car wasn't feasible, but a Vespa worked just fine. She ignored the harsh irony that Will had given her the scooter so she would never feel trapped at the house. The road was clear for a bit any direction out of the village — Will had seen to that — but soon she was dodging dead cars with rotting occupants.

She hadn't realized how accustomed she'd grown to living without being constantly surrounded by death and decay; that was Will's doing. Why he'd chosen to spend his days cleaning the mess the world had become, the little part he could control, she didn't know. But she silently thanked him.

She tried to push Will and Snickers out of her mind. She'd always been brilliant at focusing, at falling into a part and letting it absorb her. Actually, that was just according to all her paid reviews. She honestly had always thought it was difficult to be different when you had to look perpetually perfect.

So this time, the role consisted of sacrificing herself for the greater good. Well, that was extreme, but she'd certainly lessened, maybe even killed, her chance at happiness and love by leaving. Although, the nagging voice in her head reminded her, maybe there was nothing worth loving in her anymore. Maybe she didn't deserve Will, Snickers, and B.B.; maybe that white picket fence was, just as she always suspected, only for other real people.

Focus was hard to come by this day.

She'd wanted to bake cookies for Snickers — for her not just with her — like a real mom. *Peanut butter, maybe.*

She wanted to run her hand down Will's neck, across the slope of his muscled shoulder, and grasp his wrist as he was fingering her.

A family. Snickers would set the table and chat about her school day, and Will would secretly kiss her neck while she tossed the stir-fry.

They had laid a trap, probably, though not necessarily, for her; but she fell for it, literally.

FIRST THING HE SAW, IN REGARDS TO THE NOTE, was the child's yellow crayon scrawl at the bottom that read: *I go get her. Me and B.B. Not worry.* The crayons he had gotten her that first day were left behind. Snickers had always carried them in her backpack. She must have needed the room.

He read the rest of the note. He wondered why he took the time when he couldn't afford it, but he was compelled to learn Rhiannon's reasoning.

The village was empty. He had no idea how to track the girls, but he thought Big might. Big was clearly a hunter, but he wasn't an option now.

Will didn't even know where the hell Rhiannon had come from. *How could he have never asked? Time had seemed endless. No reason to rush.*

He had constructed this haven. Invited her in. She would have been safe here. He would have made sure she was safe … except … he hadn't.

He gassed a motorcycle, but then worried he would need something that would fit them all for the way back. He decided that would be a good problem to solve.

He didn't pack; he wasn't going to stop, so why would he eat or sleep? He headed out of town the way Rhiannon entered; that made some sense.

He guessed Snickers was trying to use B.B. to track Rhiannon. He'd never known that little girls were so smart, resourceful, and obstinate.

He rarely chose to, but he was so going to yell and shout and scream when he found them, hopefully together. Then he might cry, but not now.

He thought, really belatedly, that walkie-talkies might have been a good idea. Or a two-way radio, but then he'd never wanted to find people before.

Rhiannon was, at most, twelve hours ahead and likely on her Vespa, as it hadn't been parked at the house. She would've avoided the village, in case he lied about the group's intent.

Snickers must be on foot or maybe a bike; could she ride a bike? Unless… unless she was with Big. No, Big wasn't that kind of man. *But what if, what if Big wanted to get back at him? Big was a killer, not in self-defense but cold blood,* his brain maliciously echoed. *No.* He would find Snickers easily; then maybe he'd go after Rhiannon. Snickers might force his decision there, but her safety came first.

He had demanded that promise from Rhiannon, so she left, though he really wished she'd discussed it with him. This was not what he meant. He wondered if he was always destined to drive everyone away or lose people he should have held on to more fiercely.

He thought he'd stepped up.

A bug up his nose put a cap on his wallowing. He lowered his head to the wind and pushed the bike. He knew the road well.

It was three days before he set eyes on the girls again, but he never did get to yell or profess his love or even see them smile. All he really got was to hear Rhiannon's scream when Snickers went into the river.

17 / RHIANNON

HOW LONG SHE'D BEEN OUT, SHE WASN'T SURE, but it felt like days. Her head killed, and when she opened her eyes, she thought she was blind. Of course, it was just that it was night and dark, but it still took a lot of blinking to gain focus. Even then, all was blurry at the edges.

Then she remembered: the Vespa had suddenly bucked forward and thrown her. She had hoped to hit brush rather than concrete on the way down.

They must have had a wire across the road.

Her hands were tied behind her back, and her wrists felt like they'd bled already, so that wasn't good. At least her limbs were numb. That probably helped with the pain she was pretty sure she should be in. She knew almost instantly by the general lightness of her clothing that they had stripped her of every gun, knife, and even her grenades. Later on, she'd probably be pissed about losing those, but right now she was more concerned about the negative results she was getting from her internal/external wound evaluation.

She had flung her arms up to protect her face before she

hit the ground — old habits do die hard — so it didn't feel overly bruised or scraped.

A harsh kick to her right-side ribs immediately informed her that they were badly bruised, if not broken, and she stifled an agonized scream.

"I know yer awake, I saw your eyes open." She knew this voice. She wondered if he had his shotgun. She didn't feel like he'd raped her. Ah, the fucking penis; whether it worked or not, it was always about the dick. Women just didn't obsess about their clits the same way.

She cracked her eyes open again. His boots were inches away from her face, and she really hoped it wasn't her blood splattered on them. She was lying stomach down on a navy blue sleeping bag, but her cheek was currently pressed into packed dirt and embedded with small rocks.

Shotgun Asshole flipped her onto her back. It was awkward to lie on tied arms, so she tried to sit, but he pressed a boot to her belly. He hunched down, his shotgun resting on one of his thighs, to look at her. She tried to meet his gaze calmly, but the pain seeping into her arms from the increased blood flow wasn't helping.

"Was worried you wouldn't wake; that's a big bump you got on your head." He got off on her pain. "Plus, can't hurt you more if you're dead."

Rhiannon tried to retort but found her mouth too dry. Someone tried to give her water, but Asshole grabbed the canteen and gave him/her a shove. He poured the water over her head. She got a bit in her mouth, but most of it pooled between and over her breasts. He noticed, typical scum.

She refused, no matter how injured, to feel scared. She'd gotten away from Asshole before, so she would just do it again. He couldn't kill her. He saw this realization in her expression, and he raised his hand to slap her, but was grabbed by Buddy, who she could now identify, before he could.

"You know he wants her unharmed!" Buddy frantically hissed, and then looked around as if someone might be listening.

"He don't know what happened to her before we found her," Asshole countered.

"Unless she says so," Buddy reminded Asshole. Asshole didn't like advice. He shoved Buddy away, harsher than before. Buddy stumbled backwards and then wandered off to sit by the fire.

"I ain't losing no more ears over you, cunt," Asshole spit.

Rhiannon snorted and sneered. "I guess to kill me, you'll have to kill us both." Buddy, whom she'd indicated, looked up at that and shifted his handgun to rest on his knee.

"Don't listen to the bitch; she don't get it." Asshole leaned in closer like he was sharing some secret. "Let me explain. I can't do anything to you that's worse than what he's going to."

At this pronouncement, Buddy actually shuddered and wrapped his arms around himself, even though he sat a couple of feet from the fire.

"He saw you brought in," Asshole continued. "He knew who you were, then made sure everyone with you, your friends, were killed, slaughtered."

Buddy numbly finished Asshole's thought. " 'Cause then you'd know there was no help coming, nobody going to rescue you, no allies, no way out."

Asshole threw a shut-up look at Buddy, but he ignored

it to add, "Most of your group would have normally been spared, especially the females."

Buddy lapsed into silence and Asshole took up the narrative. "Then he made sure we walked you past the birth center, if you can call it that."

"He had you sit in the hole for six days with the cattle, to cut you down; had me bring my brother ..." Here his anger dimmed, and he faltered.

"The other women ... the cattle ..." She couldn't finish the question.

"Infertile, too old, they're ... feeders, for them, you know," Buddy answered.

"He's gonna do things to you I can't imagine. I hope I get to see the results." Excitement spittle formed at the edges of Asshole's lips.

"My arms are numb." She tried a play for sympathy in Buddy's direction. "One of my wrists feels broken." Buddy didn't lift his gaze from the fire.

"You don't need arms for what he wants you for," Asshole sneered. "Or legs either. You're gonna breed the Boss's Sons of New World Order. And breed and breed and breed."

He cackled and wandered over to the fire. Rhiannon's heart stopped beating, which wasn't at all helpful.

She deliberately leaned on her broken wrist, and the resulting jag of pain shocked her heart.

"Least she's awake now," Buddy muttered. "Lost us two days."

"Better than punishment for delivering her dead," Asshole reminded him as he retrieved some poor animal's leg from the fire and gnawed it.

"Hell, if she was dead, we'd have to run for it," Buddy

whined. "Bad enough returning without it, your brother, I mean. He hates losing them."

"Yeah, but we ain't going to take the blame for that." Asshole turned to smile maliciously, pieces of dead flesh between his teeth.

Rhiannon tried to ignore him as she struggled to sit up. Her movement pulled her wet T-shirt tight across her chest and drew his foul eyes again.

"I bet she was giving it up freely to that cowboy guy," Asshole pondered. "Not like she's any virgin. Boss wouldn't know the difference."

"It's your neck." Buddy shrugged.

"We could cut out her tongue, like they did in the real old days," Asshole suggested. Buddy looked at her.

"The real old days," Buddy murmured like he was actually thinking about it. Rhiannon, despite being hog-tied, tried to look as intimidating as possible.

"Nah," Buddy decided. "Boss probably wants her tongue; plus, she might bite. I hate that."

Asshole snorted, but did drop the subject of rape.

She could hear the river. They'd been on foot for half a day. Asshole and Buddy were still hoping to find motorcycles, while she looked for escape routes. They had her on a fucking chain, probably the one they'd had around It's neck. The Infected. Of course, she knew how to pick a lock; she'd played a thief once.

They had dragged her to her feet at dawn, but soon

figured out she couldn't stand yet. She buckled and heaved bile out of her empty gut.

Buddy, the idiot, had remarked, "Geesh, maybe she's really hurt. I seen her take harder falls, in that cool dragon movie, what's it called?"

"That was the stunt guy, you moron." Asshole hauled her to her feet again. "She's got a concussion; think she was faking the knocked-out part?"

Rhiannon spat remnants. Before, when she'd been unconscious, they had carted her on a gurney made from a La-Z-Boy. It was weird what you found abandoned on the side of the road, but long term, that would be impractical.

She wondered briefly if Will was tracking her, and then realized that Snickers was his priority; plus he wouldn't know which way to start. Besides, she only felt like being rescued because she was in a certain amount of pain, and she didn't think walking was going to help much.

Focus on the facts.

She was on her hands and knees at their asshole feet. They planned to enslave her as the concubine of a bigger asshole. She laughed, a little like she might slit their throats. They stopped debating movie titles. She, still laughing, locked eyes with Asshole.

She enunciated each word so that, idiot though he was, he wouldn't be confused: "Are you going to deliver me in this condition?" He, agape, stared.

"My wrist? Broken, and my ribs? Might be. My jacket? Missing, so my skin will burn like crazy. Red? Good color on me, but not as skin." The point hadn't filtered through his thick cranium, so she added, "And these cuts are going to get infected, which would be bad. Very bad."

They stared at her like maybe she was a talking dog.

They seemed thrown by her straightforwardness. She wasn't going to simper or smile.

"She's right," Buddy slowly figured. "We better fix her up. What if ... I mean ... she looks rough, nothing like that picture he, he, you know, uses?"

"Cunt! Fucking bitch!" Shotgun Asshole swore and paced. She stopped herself from smirking.

He was going to have to take care of her.

That didn't stop them from chaining her. They wrapped fabric, velvet of all things, around the neck shackle before putting it on her. They were still more scared of losing her than hurting her further, hence the chains, but they had splinted, bandaged, and tidied her up. They also had no idea who they were dealing with, and the extent she'd go to for revenge. If they managed to get her to the city, if she had to spread her legs for this psycho Boss, she was going to demand their fucking heads on a silver fucking platter.

Even though the play had fucking sucked, she'd been brilliant as Salome.

She slept only when they did, even though that was prime escape time, knowing that sleep would aid with her healing.

She woke feeling little fingers loosening the knots at her

wrists. She thought she'd known fear, but that had been nothing compared to this.

She could hear B.B.'s unmistakable breathing nearby. Her traitorous heart momentarily thrilled at the thought of being rescued by Will.

Fuck! Why would Will put Snickers in this danger? Then she realized Will wouldn't. Which meant Snickers had followed her, with B.B. *Well, that plan had harshly backfired. So, time for a new one.*

She wiggled her fingers and Snickers squeezed her hand.

Suddenly, her heart was beating like those movie drums that always signified death.

She twisted her head to try to see Snickers in the dark, to communicate fear and the need for stealth.

The chain around her neck rattled.

B.B. shifted as she sniffed down the length of the chain, which was staked about a foot from Asshole's sleeping form by the dying fire.

Snickers worked one hand loose. Holding the chain from clanking, Rhiannon fiercely hugged the girl, a gesture the child actually accepted.

She patted Snickers down and quickly inventoried a knife strapped to her leg — perhaps copying her — a shotgun across her shoulder, and a backpack.

She deliberately wrapped Snickers's hand firmly around B.B.'s collar, and held it there until she felt Snickers's nod of understanding.

Then she delicately wrapped the chain around her arm as she slid closer and closer to Asshole. He snorted and rubbed his genitals. *Typical.*

She fought the urge to strangle him with the chain and started to work on freeing the stake from the ground. They'd hammered it in with a rock.

Unexpectedly, Buddy rolled to his feet and lurched a few steps away.

Sleepwalking?

Then he unzipped and pissed. *Fuck. Not asleep, then.*

The stake pulled free from the ground with minimal noise; she must have still been pulling on it. Buddy turned around. He saw her. His eyes shifted and she was sure he was seeing a nine-year-old girl aiming a shotgun at him.

"Can she shoot that thing?" he asked quietly.

"Yep, and the dog will rip your balls off," Rhiannon return whispered. B.B. started to growl. Buddy's eyes fear-widened; he hadn't seen the dog.

"You... you going to stake him?" Buddy quavered. She inadvertently still held the stake poised over Asshole, who was now wide awake.

She was going to have to improvise their way out.

With nothing near for Snickers to brace the shotgun on, she'd get a single shot that probably wouldn't hit and would land her on her ass. Rhiannon could try to grab the gun from Snickers, but was pretty sure Buddy, and probably Asshole, would have guns trained if not fired before she could manage that move.

She mentally inventoried her injuries. *Can I run? Maybe. Can I pick up Snickers and run? No way. Were they way faster? Fuck, yes.* So they weren't going to get to walk away clean. Someone was going to get hurt, probably Snickers. She'd just be collateral damage to them.

Buddy's eyes darted toward his gun, which he'd left beside his bed. Asshole's hand twitched to reach for his own gun strapped to his leg. She was going to have to make a decision, otherwise they would, but she wasn't accustomed to having to factor the safety of other people into her choices.

Asshole moved first, just like she fucking knew he would. He reached for his gun; she stabbed the stake through his hand into the ground. He howled, but also managed to grab her neck in a chokehold with his other hand. She smashed her chain-wrapped forearm up under his chin.

Buddy dove for his gun.

She whirled around and flipped Snickers over her shoulder.

B.B. pounced and clamped down on Buddy's gun arm as he raised his hand to shoot.

She ran.

B.B. snarled and tore flesh.

Buddy screamed.

A gun went off.

Silence fell.

This lack of sound severed her heart, but she kept running. Snickers clung to her soundlessly as always. She realized she was muttering the mantra, "No, B.B., no, B.B., please no, B.B.," and stopped.

It was so dark. *Where the fuck was the moon?* So she had to stick to the road once she found it. Necessity and distance beat stealth.

Then the adrenaline infusing her brain eased, and she recognized that the river was thundering on the left. She was running the wrong way. She paused, pressed up against the cliff face, and looked back.

"Did you leave Will any clues to where you were heading?" she asked Snickers. Snickers, her face pressed against the crook of her neck, shook her head.

Fuck.

Snickers knew which direction to head because of B.B.'s nose.

She tried to not think of B.B. bleeding out, dying back there, just because she was stupid enough to get caught running away like a brat.

Rhiannon lowered Snickers, disengaged her arms from her neck, and tucked the girl behind her against the cliff, her eyes still locked on the road.

One of her ribs pressed harshly against her lung, and she willed herself to believe it was only bruised, not broken and about to puncture. Feeling through the darkness, she wiped her hands across Snickers's wet cheeks, kissed her forehead, and pulled a bobby pin from her hair. It was difficult with the dark, the angle, and without being able to see the lock, but she eventually got the neck shackle off. She wove the bent bobby pin back into Snickers's hair, retrieved the knife tied to the girl's leg, and pressed it into her hand.

Then she commandeered the shotgun and filled her pockets with shells from Snickers's backpack. She also kept the chain coiled around her arm.

Snickers painfully squeezed her shoulder, and Rhiannon looked to see a dark figure looming behind, or maybe sitting on, a boulder a dozen or so feet eastward. She didn't know how long this person had been there, but as the sun started to rise, the sky behind the figure had lightened and revealed it.

She raised the shotgun, but as the figure leaped forward, she recognized it. B.B. Snickers flung herself at the dog and B.B. whimpered.

Rhiannon pulled them into the recessed cliff spot, and

as the sun further lightened the sky, she saw that B.B. had a bullet groove across her chest.

She started to pull off her jacket to stanch the wound, but then Snickers pressed packages of gauze, bandages, and antiseptic into her hands. She had packed with forethought beyond that of a child of nine. Channeling this swell of emotion, Rhiannon smiled at Snickers, whose face lit up.

"You are simply amazing, Snickers. Thank you," she whispered, and then turned to tend B.B.'s wounds. The girl, without any fear, stood guard.

It was near dawn when she got B.B. patched and ready to go. More light meant more danger, but they couldn't stay pinned down either.

The river blocked the south, as the cliffs did the north. The city was to the west; the east led back to Asshole and Buddy, but also to Will.

"Will is going to be so pissed," Rhiannon whispered. Seeing Snickers smirk, she teased, "He's not going to be tickled pink with you, either!"

Snickers grasped her shotgun-free hand. They stepped out of their hiding spot and, skirting the cliff face, started back the way they came.

The first person they came across was not Will nor Asshole nor Buddy, but Wee Wee. She didn't instantly recognize him clothed. He grinned to display teeth that indicated he didn't get many vegetables in his fish diet. Rhiannon's first thought was to tuck Snickers behind her.

Second thought, she was pretty peeved that she hadn't heard or seen any warnings that he was nearby, such as his liberally littered leghold traps.

He tilted his head as if that offered a better angle. "I know you." He limped when he stepped closer, but unfortunately only a little.

She raised the shotgun, and that stifled his grin. He shifted right as if to see behind her, as if to see Snickers. His eyes gleamed. He had a series of fishhooks woven through his upper lip.

B.B. growled and strained against her collar, but Rhiannon continued to hold the dog firm. She didn't want to ask for trouble, hadn't asked, especially with B.B. wounded and Snickers in the mix. But she would fight, kill, if needed.

"Real familiar," he mumbled.

"You can thank me for your leg," she stated casually. "And it's really too bad the infection didn't kill you."

He grinned again, and this time, she caught something feverish in his eyes. So the infection hadn't killed him, but it had added to the crazy.

"That's a girl, ain't it?" He ignored her barb, and probably didn't get her threat either. Sometimes she was too subtle for her own good.

"A little girl is real, real valuable," he continued. "More breeding years, better chance of, of, catching, birthing multiples."

"She's just a child," Rhiannon, disgusted and disturbed, yelled and then immediately couldn't believe she was actually engaging with him at all.

"Practice makes perfect," he singsonged. "Push in, pull out, make hole big, big enough for baby, sell baby for even more than the girl!"

She had raised and fired the shotgun before she knew it. He was faster than she anticipated, and she aimed with anger, not concentration. He, even clipped by spray, rushed her and knocked her over as she was pumping the gun for her second shot. She lost the gun in the fall. She felt his hands, his skin, fever hot even through her jacket, and in their frantic tussle, she realized he was trying to bite her neck.

She rolled once, twice, and in the third roll she got her knee to his chest and tossed him off her. Momentum carried him to the cliff edge.

Snickers hesitated, knife in one hand and B.B.'s collar in the other.

Rhiannon yelled, "Run!" in the child's direction even as she charged Wee Wee, who was trying to stand. One more kick would launch him over the cliff, into the raging river and out of their lives, but a voice froze her mid-kick.

"Nope, no more running," Asshole sneered.

"And leash the dog or it'll be a bullet to the head for it and the girl," Buddy threatened.

She spun to see they had hands on Snickers, who, despite being half-off her feet, was holding B.B. from attacking the nasty new arrivals.

Wee Wee grabbed Rhiannon's leg and tried to twist her off her feet. With no momentum he couldn't manage it, so he just hung off her like a tantruming toddler. Rhiannon raised her chain-wrapped arm over Wee Wee's head; he was now chewing on her leg.

"That's enough braining for the day," Asshole ordered, and then elaborated. "Plus he's a ... a ... collaborator, yes, that's the right word —"

"Yes, very Nazi of you," Rhiannon interjected and he ignored.

"Who do you think pointed us in your direction?"

"It was the wrong direction." A weak retort, sure, but she felt the need to say something.

They stepped closer. Snickers clung to B.B.'s back with her hands acting as a muzzle. Buddy was dragging them both by the back of Snickers's belt. Asshole and Buddy had guns trained on her, but then Buddy, perhaps the smarter of the two, pressed his gun to the back of Snickers's head.

Wee Wee, now manic, started rolling and giggling. She wondered if she could knock him over the cliff edge before Asshole could stop her. She didn't get to ponder for long.

A bullet bit the dirt inches in front of Asshole's oncoming foot. They all dumbly stared at this patch of disturbed earth.

Rhiannon wondered, in the chaos that ensued, how she found the focus to notice:

The seeping — almost black — blood from Asshole's bandaged hand.

Or that Buddy wore a happy-face pin with fangs.

Or that Snickers's eyes were flecked with gold.

She saw all that — and more — in rapid-fire still images.

"Close enough," Will yelled from his cliff-top vantage. He backed this proclamation with another shot, which hit slightly to Buddy's left.

Everyone froze. But then realizing the bad guys weren't

outgunned yet, Rhiannon dove for her shotgun, only feet away in the dirt. It was the wrong choice, the wrong move, and she sure had been making more than her share of those lately.

Snickers loosened her hold on B.B., who immediately went after Asshole. Buddy grabbed for Rhiannon as Will half-ran, half-fell down the cliff.

All this strategic adult movement left Snickers defenseless against Wee Wee.

As Rhiannon grabbed and swung the shotgun on Buddy, she saw Snickers thrashing to get away from Wee Wee, who was dragging her off by one foot.

She screamed, aimed again, but didn't have time to get off a shot before Snickers had slammed her foot into Wee Wee's crotch and he crumpled. In her desperation, Snickers spun away, spun to the edge of the cliff. So near the edge, which was dry and eroded and old, that it buckled.

And Snickers fell. She twisted. The rocks underneath her feet crumbled. She fell, right off the cliff, off the cliff into the raging river below.

She didn't make a sound as she fell, her arms around her ears like a dancer, no scream, nothing. *Maybe it wasn't psychological, then, Snickers's muteness;* Rhiannon's dull brain was still making meaningless observations.

She heard someone scream, was fucking sure it was herself screaming, and someone, probably her again, blew the back of Wee Wee's head off.

She ran to the cliff edge.

She dropped the gun.

She dropped the pack off her back, Snickers's backpack and, quite simply, dove off the cliff.

Dove right off, right at the spot where Snickers had

fallen. The cliff face streaked by until the water rose up to swallow, or perhaps welcome, her.

Then the hungry, vengeful, breathtakingly beautiful river pulled her down, down into its crashing white rapids and rocky outcrops.

WILL FELT, RATHER THAN HEARD, HIMSELF scream. The second scream, "Rhiannon" — the first had been "Snickers" — felt like it shredded his throat. She had just dived off. Just ran and dived off. Like it was a sunny summer day and she needed a little cooldown, a little dip in the pool.

He recognized as he tried to run to the cliff edge that the two men, One Ear and his buddy from that, that town, turned their guns on him. They didn't shoot him, but they didn't let him get to the edge of the cliff either. Instead, they tackled him. B.B. was somehow in the mix.

He tried to crawl, but they sat, crushed his legs and dug their heels into hard-packed ground. They found holds in the rock and anchored.

His hearing came back with the roar of machine-gun fire. They cringed and covered their heads, little good that would do against bullets.

"You get off! You assholes, get the hell offa Tex!" Big swore. "Or I'll forget I recently decided to believe in the sanctity of life."

One Ear and Buddy scrambled off him.

Big, followed by ten other people with guns, shotguns and rifles, was striding in from the west.

Thus freed, Will finally got to the cliff edge, but couldn't see anything beyond rock and river.

"Clarence, go up. See if you can put eyes on them girls," Big ordered. Stupid, who apparently was Clarence, went from having his gun crammed under Buddy's eye to scampering up the cliff Will had just come down in his rescue attempt.

Big and another bearded man — Dale, according to what Big was saying — seemed to be trying to help him to his feet. But if he was going anywhere, he was going over into that river.

One Ear and Buddy were on their knees with hands on heads. Each had five guns pointed at them.

Where the hell had all these people come from?

Big seemed to be trying to soothe him by mumbling about "everything being okay" and them "figuring it all out."

Stupid yelled from the cliff top, "I see the lady!"

Will stopped struggling and turned toward Stupid's voice. So many hands were on him, so much concern in the eyes of people he didn't know. He turned to see Stupid up on the cliff. He was staring west with binoculars.

Stupid yelled again, "I see her, she's got the little girl!"

Will brushed off helpful hands and climbed the cliff.

Stupid continued to narrate, "They're riding the river feet first, like pros! No! They hit a rock, gone under."

Will's heart stopped, but his feet and hands didn't. His fingers would be bloody next time he noticed.

"Wait! No, there they are! Clinging to the rock! That

river is some bitch, but they're winning. That lady is a good swimmer, hey, Tex?"

That lady is good at everything, his numb brain offered. *I might wring her neck when I get my hands on her or at least kiss her really hard.*

"The lady looks like she's trying to get to the other side, and the girl is okay, 'cause she's clinging to the lady like shit on a log."

He realized B.B. was with him as he got near the top of the cliff. She was scrambling for footing, but the rock was crumbling underneath. She started to slip backward just as he grabbed her collar and hauled her up the last few feet. They finally stepped onto solid ground.

Stupid offered him the binoculars with an apologetic look. "They're okay, but they got swept around that bend and out of sight, see?"

Will scanned the river, following Stupid's direction, but couldn't see the girls.

"I promise, Tex, I promise they're okay," Stupid stuttered.

He felt like his brain was going to shut down, but was pretty sure this wasn't the time for a reboot. Then Big had his hand on his shoulder.

"We better get going if we're going to get to them before dusk," Big said. "Think they'll know to wait for us, know we're coming for them?"

Will laughed at that.

He laughed at the thought of Rhiannon waiting for anything, for anyone. He laughed for her unbelievable courage and for that damn dive. The look between Big and Stupid made it pretty clear they thought he was going insane. So he stopped laughing and started giving orders.

He was pretty sure they'd been waiting for him to wake up and take charge for a while now.

SHE SLICED THROUGH THE WATER, AND WITHIN the peaceful grip of the thundering river, she momentarily thought about not surfacing at all. She could just surrender ... life was such an endless fight, a constant struggle to move and do and consume and try, try to just be, to exist.

She thought of Snickers, who was too young to be overwhelmed in all of this. And then her legs moved, kicked against the demanding water. She panicked that she wasn't going to break free, that she'd waited too long, let the current have its way and signed over her life rights.

She broke through and pulled air into her deflated lungs. Her rib was still stuck, maybe broken, but she had other things to worry about. Such as the insane speed with which she was being dragged and the jutting, jagged rocks that she was lucky she hadn't yet hit headfirst. Instructions from a river-rafting trip taken with her father in her teens came to her, and she faced downriver and stuck her legs forward. Her father had died a few weeks after that trip. By his own hand. She stuffed that memory away for another dark day.

She let the current direct her, as she was sure it had directed Snickers. Scanning, she squinted against the sun. She'd lost her sunglasses. Everything was white. White water surrounded and pulled her around rocky outcrops. Snickers's dark hair had to show against all this white.

If Snickers had made it to the surface ... if ... if ... if, her brain nagged. *The river was so strong and Snickers was so little.*

The river twisted and she scraped her leg on something jagged underneath the surface. *At least there weren't any sharks in a river.* She hadn't realized before how cold the water was — *cold and clear — good enough to drink.*

She suddenly dropped a few feet and went under; when she surfaced again, she found herself in a sort of resting place. *A pool drop,* her brain unhelpfully supplied.

Going under the water brought her to her senses again and... *there!*

A scarf tied around a rock?

She swam to the other side of the calm pool. She wedged up against a boulder so the river didn't drag her up and over the next set of rapids. Then, tracing the scarf, she found Snickers.

The girl had tried to anchor to the rock, but was now hanging on to the ends of the scarf and barely keeping her head out of the water.

Rhiannon wrapped her legs around her side of the rock and reached over to drag Snickers back. The river wasn't too happy about releasing the girl.

Snickers's lips and hands were blue-tinged, and her head rolled limp. She seemed unaware of being pulled over and wedged against the boulder.

Rhiannon fumbled with the scarf and the knots that

Snickers had made around her wrists. The constant pull of the current had painfully tightened those knots.

Only when blood rushed back into Snickers's hands did she react, and the girl's pained, ferocious look gradually eased into recognition and ... *joy*?

"Hey, baby." Rhiannon smiled and almost got a return smile. "What a ride! But maybe now is a good time to dry off?"

Snickers nodded her agreement.

She looked for a place to climb out of the river, but saw none nearby.

"Looks like we might need to go downriver farther. You up for it?"

Snickers nodded and tried to climb around onto her back, but couldn't seem to move or grip very well with her right arm. *Was it broken?* Snickers didn't seem to be bleeding and she saw no jutting bone, but given the way the girl was moving, it was at least painful.

"Sorry, baby, this might hurt. Try arms around my neck, legs like this." She coached Snickers until she was wrapped around her frontways.

Then, fingers clumsy with cold, she tied one end of the scarf to Snickers's belt and one end to her own, and hoped that was the right choice.

The child didn't make a sound, but Rhiannon felt her desperately clenched limbs and her fierce little heart pounding against her breastbone.

As she eased around the rock and let the current catch them, she realized she wasn't scared anymore. With Snickers, she could accomplish anything.

She tried to steer toward a group of rocks and hoped for another calm pool. But instead of a safe haven, she found a sinkhole in disguise. They went under, but rather than fighting and getting confused, she shielded Snickers as best she could and let the river have its way. They tumbled over and over. Her back smashed against a rock, and for a while, direction had no meaning.

Then they bobbed to the surface.

She needed both arms to grab another rock, so she had to trust that Snickers could hang on. Then she coughed up a lungful, as did the girl.

More eruptions of white water rose ahead of them, which could indicate drops or pools or rocks. After those, the river veered around a wicked bend.

She stayed as close to the left as the river would allow. Though it was the wrong side, it was closest, and Snickers had to get out of the cold. Will was on the opposite side, if he even thought to try to find them. He might assume them dead. She hoped not, for Snickers's sake, of course.

Unable to actually feel her numb legs as they scrambled against the smooth river rock, Rhiannon finally managed to pull them partly up on shore. She collapsed, half in the water, and took an involuntary nap. She woke with frozen legs, but her body, curled around Snickers, was warm.

Some of the hair on her forehead lifted in the breeze, so she'd been out long enough for it to partially dry. Thankfully it wasn't winter.

She tried to sit, but Snickers was way heavy out of the water. Careful of the girl's arm, she shifted her off and crawled farther onto shore.

Snickers, curled into a fetal position with her eyes

squeezed shut, started to violently shiver, yet her forehead was oddly warm. Hot, even. Trying to not freak about hypothermia and/or strange fevers, Rhiannon simply gathered the girl into her arms and held on until the shaking eased. As she rocked Snickers, she kept her eye on the northern clifftop. If Will was coming for them, and he'd be hours behind, he'd appear there.

Later, when Snickers seemed a little more stable, she gathered dry leaves and some wood. Thankful for the waterproof matches Snickers had tucked into a jacket pocket from her backpack, she lit a fire.

Using the scarf as a bandage, Rhiannon splinted Snickers's arm. She contemplated humming a soothing lullaby and discovered she didn't know any. She made an effort to talk; it was too easy to fall silent around Snickers.

"That hurts, hey, love?" she asked. "We'll get you painkillers."

She found she was staring at the cliff again. Snickers followed her gaze.

"Maybe Will saw us in the river; he and B.B. might be coming."

The girl softly stroked the back of her hand as if to comfort her, and she felt so incompetent. Wasn't she supposed to be the adult here?

"We'll wait here for a bit more. The fire almost has your clothing dry, but we're going to get hungry. I ... I ... dumped the pack," she rambled. "I'm going to look for some berries or —"

Snickers grabbed her arm, tighter than Rhiannon would've imagined her capable, as she tried to stand.

"Okay. No berry hunting. Here, turn your back to the fire now. I don't know how we're going to get your jacket back on over that splint. Maybe we'll have to switch; let's see if yours fits me."

Snickers actually smiled when she couldn't get the sleeve halfway up her arm.

Then she tried to fit her foot into Snickers's still-soggy shoe and almost got a silent laugh for her clowning. She'd never been funny before.

All that joy drained away from the girl's face as a hard metal point was pressed against Rhiannon's neck. Snickers's eyes flicked to multiple points behind her back. She couldn't tell if it was a rifle or gun, but it didn't much matter, as both would certainly blow her head off, especially at this range.

They seemed to have come out of nowhere, but probably drawn by her voice, they had just stepped a couple of feet out from the forest border.

She could tell they knew who she'd been in her previous life, and that they'd been looking for her, just by the exchanged glances and congratulatory smiles.

She looked across at the cliff again: still empty. Then she looked upriver, both sides, as far as she could, to reconfirm that there was no rescue coming this time.

A man with glasses stepped out from behind two others, both of whom had their clumped hair streaked bright red, but with paint, not dye. Even the man who hunkered by Snickers and reached for her broken arm had wide streaks of red paint slashed across his jacket and bag.

Snickers shied away.

"I'm a doctor," he offered. First to Snickers, then

getting no response, he turned to Rhiannon to repeat, "I'm a doctor."

"The medical bag kind of gave you away. A backpack would be more suitable, what with the forest hiking and then random patching of people."

He thought about this, too seriously, for a bit, and then replied, "Yes, but appearances still matter in this world, as you will soon learn."

She didn't get what he meant, but never did like asking for clarification. She always preferred to interpret, and in this instance, she was still gathering facts.

"I'm here. Would you let the doctor look at your arm?" she asked Snickers.

Snickers acquiesced, but kept her eyes glued to Rhiannon's own. The gun stopped pressing against the junction between her skull and her spine.

"They're wet," a voice directed, and clothing was piled nearby.

"Musta come out of the river," someone shrilled. "That's why we missed 'em on the way. Odd, ain't it, for someone like her to be in a river?"

No one replied.

She could almost feel tension leap through the group. She counted seven — no, nine — of them, all variously streaked with red and carrying an assortment of weapons. Mostly they were outfitted with hunting rifles. She wondered why no one other than the doctor had spoken to her, but as she didn't want to be the instigator, she chose to just listen.

The doctor wrapped Snickers's arm with a Tensor and fashioned a sling. He offered painkillers, which the girl refused. He didn't seem to care.

"Just 'cause she ain't all painted and pretty, don't mean

I don't recognize her properly. She's the one he wants," the shriller continued.

When he, the one who'd ordered the dry clothing, stepped closer, she saw he wore his red paint in eleven bands on each upper sleeve. And, now that she'd noticed, others had bands as well, but no one else had as many. *Were they for identification or hierarchy within the group?*

He actually tilted her chin up to look at her face. He squinted as if trying to see differently, and then grunted in approval and moved away.

"So you're not him, then? Him with the billboards, the monster pets, and baby mills?" she guessed. "And you have a group name, red something?"

A quiver that could have been laughter reverberated through the group, but he ignored her questions with another grunt. She shifted closer to Snickers.

The cliff was still empty.

"Get her on her feet. I want to be in the city before dawn and ready for our reward," Grunt ordered with a grin.

This time the group did laugh, but not like he'd told a joke. More like in anticipation of a hard-won victory; the backslapping helped sell it.

"And the girl?" the doctor, who wasn't overtly amused, asked.

"I don't care. Bring her. Leave her." Grunt squatted to dig through a bag.

She wrapped an arm around Snickers and started looking for nearby weapons and escape routes.

"She might be useful later," the doctor suggested.

Grunt found what he was looking for in the bag, a couple of PowerBars, and he whipped them at her. She snatched them both in one hand. He was pleased.

She, wanting to wipe the smug off, said, "We're not

going anywhere with you," but this only seemed to make his grin wider.

"You think you got a choice? Nine of us and you with no gun? Even the doctor's killed for our cause." He didn't grunt when he threatened.

She hated when they used words like "choice," "cause," and "kill" in one breath. They might as well wear "I'm 100% Pure Psychopath" T-shirts.

"You're the golden goose, lady," he said. "You're our vehicle to freedom, our Trojan horse. So you're going to get on your feet, quickly. You're going to walk, not run. You're not going to talk or ask questions, because nobody here gives a shit what you think or feel or want. And you're going to do this by the count of three; otherwise I'll tear the girl's head right off her scrawny little useless shoulders. One."

She stood, with no argument or fight, because she'd just figured out that their red paint was like a gang tag, and the armbands denoted kills. And according to his red paint armbands, Grunt had killed twenty-two people. Whether that was before or after the virus had devastated humanity, she didn't care. She wasn't about to add Snickers to his list.

She reached down to bring Snickers to her feet, wincing when her rib made friendly with her lung again. Twisting to the right wasn't a good idea.

Grunt nodded to the doctor, which propelled him to step in for an examination.

"Don't want your hands anywhere near me," she growled.

"You don't have a choice." He pitched his voice low. "If you're hurt, he'll want you fixed. You won't be allowed to be less than perfect."

"Great, just like surviving my teens with my mother,"

she muttered back, but he didn't smile. Her charm had no traction with these people. He cut off her T-shirt when she wouldn't raise her arms. No one ogled her, which was oddly discomforting.

As the doctor slid his hands over her ribs and torso, the others, not even remotely interested in her or Snickers, broke up into small groups to talk quietly.

"I don't understand," she asked, "why a child isn't more valuable to them. A female." But the doctor just turned away to speak with Grunt.

The sun was definitely setting now, and Rhiannon knew that Will would never be able to track them across the river and through the woods in the dark. Nevertheless, she still glanced back, once more, at the cliff. Her heart skipped to see people, multiple people, looking down at them. She wanted to raise her hand, but was worried that waving would draw attention. She shouldn't have worried; the bad guys had already seen the new arrivals.

Guns were quickly raised and aimed, not to shoot with, but for the scopes. Attempting to hit targets across the expanse of the river with the sun setting behind them would just be a waste of ammo.

The doctor hastily crossed back with a large Tensor bandage to wrap tightly around her ribs. "Cracked or broken, this'll help," he offered. She pulled on one of the donated sweatshirts. Its logo declared her to be a student of the University of British Columbia.

Then Grunt was by her side.

"They with you?" he asked, and she shrugged. He then grabbed her chin and cranked it in the direction of the cliff.

"They looking for you?" he menaced.

"No," she spat, "there's too many of them to be —" But then she saw B.B., so that must be Will up there.

Grunt watched her closely, seeing what she knew the moment she thought it. He dropped her chin and heaved Snickers up over his shoulder.

She shrieked and tried to throw herself on him, to tear Snickers away, but the others surrounded and contained her before she got near.

Grunt strode off into the trees, with Snickers just looking back.

"Move, lady. Follow the man; he won't hurt the girl," Shriller explained.

The remainder of the group, including the doctor, gathered their gear and followed the leader.

She paused to take a last look at the cliff.

She cupped her hands around her mouth and yelled, "Will!" He was far enough away that she couldn't really identify him, but he raised his hand.

Then she turned to follow the others into the dense forest. A quick jog placed her behind Grunt. She touched Snickers's forehead. Grunt didn't glance back or slow.

RHIANNON TURNED TO RUN OFF AFTER THE GROUP that had snatched Snickers. There was no way to follow; Will was pinned on this side of the river. They'd only made it this far, this fast, because Big had vehicles parked near where Snickers and Rhiannon had gone in the river. The river was a far more direct and quicker route to the city than the roads.

"All right then." He turned to rally the group of eight, including One Ear and Buddy, who had followed him here. "We keep on moving upriver."

Big stepped up beside him and patted B.B.'s head. She was still staring alertly after Rhiannon and Snickers. Stupid stood a ways back.

"They ain't going to kill them," Big said.

"There's worse things than dying," Will retorted as he lowered the binoculars to side-glance at Big.

"Yup, I figure they both been through worse things already. But now they got you," Big continued. "You can't sneak in to the city, Tex."

"If ... if the city is where they're going."

"Clarence and I know 'em," Big said. "That red paint shit is hard to miss. They see themselves as sort of freedom fighters, 'cept they ain't actually on our side."

"Doesn't concern me," Will replied. He couldn't stand more yammering. Rhiannon, Snickers, danger: end of discussion. "I'll go alone," he said. "You have no obligation, Big."

Big snorted and pointed westward, deep into the valley. "You ain't going to easily find her in there without help or without major guns." As dusk deepened, clusters of lights glowed in derelict skyscrapers that punctuated the cityscape. They, whoever they were, had electricity. "First, it's a big place. Second, I hear they got some sort of civil war going on," Big persisted.

"Where'd you hear that, Big?" Will sighed.

"People just have a way of talking around me, Tex." Big grinned and glanced back at Stupid, who now held One Ear and Buddy on their knees. Both hostages looked very roughed up. Stupid prompted One Ear with an ass kick.

"Yeah, yeah, that's them with the red paint," One Ear spat. "Worse than us by far. They got no reason. We're rebuilding humanity. We got rules. The girl means nothing to them."

"Then why take Rhiannon and Snickers?" Will's voice actually shook with anger. One Ear didn't answer until Stupid's kick prompted him again.

"It don't get more famous than Rhiannon Wells unless the Queen of England was immune, and who'd want to fuck her?" One Ear blurted.

Will turned his back and felt anger burn through to his clenched fists. *She was just a damn prize!*

Then Big, real quiet, laid it out for him. "This is them I talked about, Tex. Them who take our women in raids. All women — hell, any person — has a right to decide who, where, and when."

"And what exactly do you suggest, Big?" If he needed their help to rescue Rhiannon and Snickers, he might as well know the fallout cost now.

"Guns, big guns, people who can use them, and you. I got a feeling you got lots of good ideas on offensive play. I figure we just stop 'em." Will didn't respond so Big continued. "I know you think what we were before don't matter, that it's how we behave in the present that counts. You taught me that, Tex, though I had to think about it for a bit. But we do each got skills, put enough of us together and we have a... a..."

"Community?" Stupid suggested.

"Yes, I was going to say family, but that's better, Clarence," Big agreed, then concluded, "You lead, we go."

"Just to clarify. You want me to help you build an army, lead you to war with these Rebuild Humanity guys, and you'll help me find and rescue the girls."

"That about covers it." Big grinned.

"And, just because somehow you've figured out I played pro football some time ago, you think I'm some sort of strategist?" Will asked.

"Saw you throw. Damn shame about that knee of yours, but it's always the knee with quarterbacks, ain't it?" Big mused.

"Yup," Stupid agreed.

"Course, we didn't recognize you right away, but when we decided we were tired of trouble, we knew to come to you," Big explained further. "We'll help you get your girls back. We just want to do it smart, and you got the brains and the organizing skills."

Will took a moment to look at the river, which he could

now hear more than see as night darkened the valley quicker than the mountain sky.

"We need to regroup," he said finally, deciding.

"That we do," Big agreed.

"One Ear knows the city like the back of his hand, don't you?" It was a statement, not a question.

"Maybe," One Ear begrudgingly answered.

Stupid grabbed hold of his one remaining ear and growled, "Don't ya remember our chat? And how you decided to answer all our questions?"

"Yeah, I know the city. I helped pick it. I helped him set everything in motion. He's a visionary, you know." One Ear seemed actually proud.

Big snorted at this statement. "We ain't fans of visionaries, are we, Clarence?"

"Nah. Seems like there's an awful lot of that going around. Maybe the virus does something to some people's brains even when it don't kill 'em?" Stupid pondered.

Will arrived at his first strategic decision. "You, Buddy, you're going to the city."

Buddy freaked. "Boss'll kill me, coming in without her."

"You aren't going in without Rhiannon; you're following her and her kidnappers. That ought to be valuable information," he suggested.

"And what's to stop me from telling him your plans?" Buddy threatened.

"Tell him anything you want; what do you know?" Will shrugged.

"That you're coming for them, that they're important to you, that you've got others with you, and you're coming from the east," Buddy answered.

"Don't suppose it matters. Unless your boss has the

girls, and if he does, that'll make them easier to find. Won't it, One Ear?" he prodded.

"So, Boss'll rescue Rhiannon and the kid from the Red Jackets, and then you think you can just follow some map drawn by him to get to them." Buddy, still sneering and sarcastic, jutted his chin at One Ear.

"Well, except for the map part, no one can read them properly anyway, that sounds like the beginnings of a real plan, Tex!" Big was beyond pleased.

"Plus a bullet to your brain will make it real hard to talk," Stupid piped up.

"Right, I'll be so scared of you when I'm in the city," Buddy spit.

"You will, seeing as I'll always be close enough to be holding a gun to ya." Stupid turned to Will. "I do brainstorming, Tex. I was good at that part of school."

He was happy for Stupid's support. He'd never been a good bully, but he had serious doubts about this new plan.

Stupid continued before he could interject. "Say I'm Buddy's new best friend, saved him from the river when One Ear met his death? He don't go nowhere without me."

Buddy wasn't buying. "Your threats are nothing compared to the Boss. I go to the city? I talk. You have Stupid here come with me? I get him killed."

Buddy was right. It wasn't a safe play, no matter how much he wanted to send help after the girls right now, right away. Too many things that could go wrong. Stupid watched him closely and saw denial on his face before it made it to his lips.

"I got a lot to atone," Stupid solemnly stated. "I figure I make sure the ladies are safe till you can get 'em, that might square me a bit."

"But you got no real way of keeping Buddy in line,

Clarence. Even if you did manage to shoot him if he opened his mouth, you'd be sacrificing yourself."

Big was nodding his head in agreement. Stupid looked devastated. Buddy looked a little too smug.

"No. Our choices are to kill him, keep him, or let him go. Keeping two hostages is just asking for trouble, and killing isn't something to be casual with."

"I got ya, Tex." Stupid wasn't happy about it, but he seemed to be listening. "Course" — Stupid turned to leer at Buddy — "there're worse things than dying."

Will almost laughed at Stupid's perseverance. Instead he just asked them to give him a bit of time to think; then he walked back to the vehicles. Stupid seemed happy to watch over the hostages, and Big tagged along to rally the troops.

He needed paper. Big was right; he had always been good at strategy. Course, Xs and Os now represented guns and death, so that was new.

SHE DIDN'T LIKE WALKING IN THE DARK, surrounded by creepy people she didn't know, and separated even by a shoulder from Snickers. She'd catch a flash of the whites of the girl's eyes every time the moon angled through the trees just right, and knew that she was okay. Still, Rhiannon stayed on high alert, maybe because no one spoke directly to them, maybe because she knew they were headed toward the city. As long as they stayed to this side of the river — she could hear it to the right — they were far enough away to have a chance of escaping.

A brief muttering rumbled back through the group. She walked face-first into Grunt's back and smashed her nose. He had stopped suddenly.

Now that she was within reach, Snickers quickly wrapped her unbroken arm about Rhiannon's neck, and miracle — Grunt allowed the girl to shift off his shoulder and into her achingly empty arms. Not wanting to alarm Snickers further, she attempted to not clutch her, but failed miserably.

Grunt turned sideways, and she realized they had flashlights; she just hadn't been able to see before beyond his bulky back. She had never liked bulky-muscled guys. A long, lean build like Will's, now that was perfect. Not so tall that you cranked your neck to kiss, but tall enough to feel — *protected*. Plus, guys who obsessed about their bodies were usually assholes, like Grunt, who now grabbed her upper arm and yanked her sideways.

He pulled Rhiannon and Snickers, who was still clinging to her, off the path and through some trees until they came to a small clearing. Here, a few others she hadn't seen before were guarding a low concrete building. The door was hanging off its hinges, but from violence, not age; the hut-like structure was old but well maintained.

Grunt switched from pulling to pushing her toward the building. She dug in her heels. Why should she go in there? It didn't lead anywhere as far as she could see.

"Get in, climb down," Grunt ordered. Three flashlight beams swung to light the inside of the building, and she saw a ladder leading down. Shriller, as if he'd been waiting for this moment his entire life, scampered down the ladder; so she decided it was safer, relative to the current kidnapping at gunpoint, to follow than negotiate.

Setting Snickers down from the perceived safety of her arms was a struggle. She momentarily worried that Grunt would step in and forcefully remove the girl, but he didn't.

While climbing down, she glanced around the area lit by the flashlights' beams and wondered if she'd missed her chance at escaping. She thought this might be a sort of mechanical room, though its location in the middle of a forest seemed very odd. The raised letters on the first rung read GVRD. As she descended, farther and farther, she realized where this was all heading. They were using the old sewers to move in and out of the city — and she guessed — under the river.

Fuck.

She wasn't claustrophobic, but —

She stepped down once more and hit ground. Snickers, who had climbed down after, crawled from the ladder into her arms without touching down.

Rhiannon turned to see Shriller, flashlight in hand, waiting at the opening to one of three tunnels. She'd have to bend in half to crawl through.

"Don't worry, no poo poo, just used for overflow, except no chance of that now!" Shriller found the death of 99.9 percent of the population funny.

More people climbed down the ladder, so she had to move. She didn't bother darting off into one of the other sewer lines, like her character would have in a movie. In fact, she was surprised they could move around undetected like this anyway; *shouldn't you always check the sewers when hunting people?* Seeing her look, Grunt grinned. It wasn't comforting.

"These are old, unmapped, but my gramps was a city planner back when they were laid."

It was a little disconcerting that he could read her thoughts like that; scary, actually. She'd always been considered a bit of an enigma.

"Don't go thinking to pretend you're claustrophobic; I know you aren't." Grunt was back to snarling orders, and as punctuation he gave her a short shove forward.

She briefly wondered what they were going to do to her once they got her into the city. She tamped down that train of thought quickly. If it hadn't been obvious before, it was now. *Guessing the future was pointless; you dealt with what you could at the given time and gave up on the impossible.*

Good thing that very little got slotted into the impossible category... of course, this day was far from over.

Grunt knocked her shoulder with his to communicate he wasn't pleased with daydreaming. Evidently, he'd never fully learned to use his words.

After a few cramped steps, Rhiannon, with prompting from her bruised ribs, realized she wasn't going to be able to carry Snickers much farther.

She fished the scarf from around Snickers's neck and tied the ends around each of their wrists. That way, they couldn't be easily separated.

Water dripped. She could hear it even over the sounds of people breathing nearby. Areas around the soldered bolts — *or maybe they were called rivets* — looked wet. She really, really, really tried to not think about the thousands of pounds of pressure placed by the river on these old, old, old pipes. Not thinking about it didn't fix it, but dwelling never made anything easier. Plus, it wasn't as if she had any control over their location.

She wondered if the commuting rats bothered Snickers, but the girl didn't flinch; others, farther back, were more vocal until Grunt yelled.

Her mind wandered; the lack of visual input didn't help her focus. She wondered how many blows to the head one person could recover from.

Weren't there brain pathways, which, once severed, never regrew? Did they compensate, perhaps never the same, but not noticeably different? Is it possible that I am actually suffering some massive delusion? Why does it always come round to that thought, that I could actually be concocting this all in my mind? She tried to remember if she'd been hit on the head before the virus.

Snickers's quick hand squeeze focused the drift of her mind. Raised, perhaps concerned voices and more flashlight beams emanated from up ahead.

She stepped from the sewer into another mechanical room; more red-streaked people were here. One, a woman, was familiar, excepting the red hair. Though it could just be that the woman was actually looking her in the eye, when the others, rudely, didn't look at her or Snickers at all. Her brain started clicking around this observation, as it was currently prone to doing. *Maybe they weren't not looking out of rudeness... maybe they weren't looking at us because they didn't want to form any connection. Fuck, what the fuck are they going to do with us?*

The familiar woman stepped forward to address Grunt as he stepped from the sewer pipe. She laid her hand on his arm and leaned in to talk. She couldn't hear what the woman said, and Grunt wasn't happy about the message, but he turned his angry look on her rather than the messenger.

So I'm the sacrificial lamb here, am I? The one who you blame when things go wrong. The one that you punish —

"You know me." The familiar woman spoke as if she was pissed she had to state the obvious.

"I do?" Rhiannon answered, not giving an inch, or even a shit, really.

"I've done your makeup for, like, over three hundred thirty-five days in the last ten years and you don't recognize me?" The woman seemed overly attached to numbers and facts.

Fuck.

Mandy.

Now she could see past the red-painted, dreadlocked hair and the ten-years-too-old look you got from lack of fresh veggies.

"You counted?" Rhiannon smiled when sarcastic, a habit picked up from romantic comedies; even if she was a bitch, she always had to be fuckable. Though more often, she played a dull simpleton, but, of course, you still either wanted to be her or to fuck her. It was her life's work up to now.

"Take the girl," Mandy ordered.

She screamed then, right in their faces, when they reached for Snickers. She screamed all her anger, frustration, and tears she couldn't cry. This inhuman sound ripped through the small space, reverberated along, and echoed from the sewer tunnels. They cringed and covered their ears. They were all looking now. She'd scared them. They saw she was a real, breathing, feeling person. They'd heard her fear of losing the child.

But not Mandy; she stepped forward as the others stumbled back, and laid a perfectly manicured clawlike hand on Snickers's shoulder.

"I'm not interested in your current drama, Rhiannon," Mandy purred. "The child means nothing; we have a different role for you to play."

Snickers bit Mandy. Not a how-do-you-do nip, but a

full-on, mouth-full-of-blood chomp. She just turned her head and latched onto Mandy's wrist. Mandy shrieked — a sound no way as impressive as her feral scream had been, but earsplitting nonetheless — and tried to shake Snickers off.

"That's icky, Snickers; you never know where makeup people have been!" Rhiannon jokingly chided the child all the while holding her close.

The others hesitated. She wasn't going to hurt Snickers by trying to tear her head away, so she simply punched Mandy in the nose. More blood spurted. Mandy reeled back into the approaching crowd, as crowded as a ten-by-twenty room can get.

She hitched Snickers onto her back and tried to skirt around the wall. There were too many of them. She wasn't even going to get to the entrance of a sewer let alone into one.

So Snickers was ripped from her.

They were still tethered by the scarf, which their attackers didn't figure out too quickly; but then they pinned them, side-by-side, on the ground. She thrashed and fought.

"Not her face!"

"Not her face!"

Now where had she heard that before? *Ha. Life was just one big oval running track.*

In the end, they all just laid on her. Her ribs shifted and she couldn't help but moan in pain. She discerned the doctor's concerned face in the crowd. He was talking to Grunt.

Snickers, characteristically, didn't make a sound. Rhiannon could see her trying to make eye contact; she was always big with the eye contact.

She wasn't going to cry. Fuck, she was so fucking tired of telling herself that! They'd have to kill her to keep her away from Snickers.

Grunt, along with Mandy, who pinched her gushing nose while the doctor tended her bleeding wrist, loomed over her. Grunt had a big knife. She tried to flex, but they had her spread-eagle on the concrete; one person pinned each limb. The scarf was cutting off the circulation to her hand.

Grunt, threatening the only physical link she had to Snickers, slipped his knife under the silk scarf, but Mandy placed her hand on his back.

"Rhiannon, you let the girl go willingly, or I'll have dear Dean cut off her hand. Then we'll leave her trapped in the sewers to bleed out and die."

Grunt glanced at Mandy like he didn't like the sound of that; but then, he looked back and she could see he was resolved. She heard muttering among the group, but no one spoke out when Grunt shifted the position of the knife to hover over Snickers's tiny wrist.

She locked eyes with Snickers and marveled at the trust that emanated from that gaze. "No point in you losing a hand, is there?" she asked. Snickers shook her head.

"Get off my fucking arm," she swore at the guy on her left arm. He backed off as if she was poison; maybe she was. She reached for the knot on her wrist, but met Snickers's eye before she untied it.

"No one hurts you and lives to talk about it —" Rhiannon vowed.

"That's enough," Mandy snapped.

"And if it's Mandy in my way, she dies first." She continued as if she hadn't been interrupted, and then undid the knot. Snickers actually smiled. Rhiannon didn't have time — or, honestly, the need — to second-guess the moral implications and complications of vowing vengeance kills to a child.

They, maybe three or four people, pulled Snickers away into a sewer tunnel. The girl reached for her until she was engulfed in darkness.

Mandy snorted a laugh. "Touching. Let's hope you can use those acting skills for good and not just profit."

They hauled her to her feet.

"Mandy," Rhiannon sneered. "Didn't recognize the face, but your ass is impossible to mistake. Too bad your new life hasn't helped with that."

Mandy's face mottled under her layer of shellac, and her mouth, fishlike, sucked air. Makeup people were always easy to put in their place.

Rhiannon capped the insult as she smoothed her own always-perfect hair. "Nice boots. Not as fine as the ones I gave you last Christmas, but easier, I see, to clean of innocent blood."

"Let's go. It's going to take hours to fix her face." Mandy tried to get this last word in by turning to lead the way down a tunnel across from the one they'd carried Snickers through.

This pathetic insult didn't hit the vanity mark Mandy was hoping for; but it did make her worry what, exactly, they needed of her face.

ONCE AGAIN, HE SHOULD HAVE KNOWN BETTER than to leave things unsaid. It took a few hours before they'd figured out that Buddy and Stupid were missing, and by then, it was too late and too dark to turn back to find them. One Ear was more than happy to direct them to the note that Stupid had left in his pocket, but it was Big, who knew something of Stupid's mind, who offered clarification.

"He musta figured that you'd never send him on a suicide mission, but redemption won out over caution. I doubt he figures he's disobeying orders; rather I'd guess he sees it as a secret mission of sorts."

Secret mission. Damn.

They'd needed to source more vehicles for the trip back, and while getting them fueled, Will had been bent over his little pieces of paper, scratching out strategy, when Stupid had wandered over and asked him questions about Snickers and Rhiannon. He half remembered talking about strawberry plants and yellow crayons. Now Stupid had secret passwords for his secret mission and wasn't nearly as dim as he seemed. All Will could do now was pray that Stupid managed to stick to Buddy like glue and that Buddy valued his own life over revenge. He also had to admit that it settled him a bit, knowing that someone on the girls' side was going to be in the city. If Stupid didn't die before getting there.

They drove through the night. Near dawn, they caught up with the remainder of Big's group, who had reached the open plain and stopped to wait. Not needing to track the girls, like Will had on the way out, had made the return trip quicker. He hoped that ease of speed stuck with him when he headed back to the city.

They all called him Tex with deference if they spoke at all, like they knew him; when he didn't want to eat or sleep, they kept pace.

B.B. was in the back of Big's pickup, but, afraid that she would try to head back for Rhiannon and Snickers, Will kept close to her on the motorcycle. This was probably unnecessary, as B.B. seemed pretty occupied with keeping the hog-tied One Ear, who was also in the pickup, scared shitless. If One Ear even squirmed, B.B. let loose one of her rippling snarls. She took guard duty seriously; the loss of the girls must have been confusing. He tried to not think about that. He dwelled on breaking every barrier between them and him instead. If there wasn't already a path, he'd make one.

By midday, they'd hit the outskirts of his town — or

rather, Textown — as he'd heard the others whisper. Here, their group started expanding.

As singles or small groups, on foot or cycles, new people seemed to be heading toward town. His bigger group just absorbed them as they passed. Each time they gained more people, Big's grin looked to split his face, and though hazardous to his driving, he never put down the CB radio. Oddly, these newcomers all sought him out; some ran, touched him, and called him Tex, and some just watched as he passed, and then followed. It was always the same: the newcomers would turn to see them barreling up the road behind, and... well, they didn't exactly smile, but relief flooded their faces. First, it was one, then two, then ten new people. It was Big's doing, but he — he as in Tex — was to be some sort of nominated figurehead.

They were thirty strong when they reached town, and more new people mixed with Big's group here, too many to immediately count.

They had claimed houses, but seemed to be waiting outside for their arrival. He saw children and women. One woman was actually pregnant.

B.B. barked in a way he'd never heard, and Will turned in time to see the answering bark from a chocolate lab that seemed to be guarding a boy. And he realized that for all his foraging, stocking, and restoring, the town had just been missing people. It needed a purpose, as he had.

Then he saw the tank.

It was parked in front of the hotel. He stopped his motorcycle to stare. Big pulled the pickup alongside. Will couldn't help but laugh. The green of the tank stood in sharp contrast to the brightly painted quaint hotel and houses. He had always thought tanks were gray.

"Well, Big," he mused, "you did mention something about needing guns."

Big laughed and added, "And people who know how to use them."

A man who'd been lounging on one of the tank wheel tracks jumped down when he saw them approach.

"Boomer," Big introduced. "Boomer, Tex."

A peculiar hush fell along the street; engines were silenced, and all turned to look at him. Boomer saluted and only then shook Will's hand.

B.B. jumped down from the pickup and, despite the presence of the lab, moved to flank him.

"Does the tank have a name?" he feebly joked.

"I call her Delilah." Boomer nervously twisted his kerchief.

"Good name; hopefully she cuts our Samson down to size," Will awkwardly praised.

Dale, one of Big's lieutenants, stepped over to take the motorcycle from him, and he was suddenly very happy to not have its extra weight.

A voluptuous woman forced the crowd on the hotel veranda to part as she hustled toward them; Big stepped to pick her up with a whoop and then offered an introduction: "Luanne has generously agreed to share my bed till she tires of me." Luanne giggled and swatted Big's chest.

Everyone seemed to be waiting on something, and he had a sinking feeling that something was him.

"Luanne, is there enough food and beds?" he asked.

"Hell yeah, Tex. You got this town stocked and then some. We much appreciate the hospitality. More people arrive every hour."

"I think Big has been sending them our way," Will stated.

Big nodded. "We're going to need an army, and these people are ready to fight."

"Tex, Big says you're going to stop them who took my sister," Luanne said. "Yes, I know it was odd that we both were immune, but is it true?"

"I'm going to try," was all he would promise; but, not minding his lack of commitment, she gave him a peck on his cheek before she sashayed off.

Big hungrily watched Luanne as she hustled back to the hotel, and Boomer shifted his feet like he wished he could just get back to the tank. Will guessed it was time to take charge, but he wasn't sure where to start. What he really wanted was to get in the tank and head back to the city.

"Boomer, we got more firepower than just the tank?"

"Sure thing, Tex." Boomer's eyes sparkled like he was talking about his children.

"Well," Will thought out loud, "guess town hall is as good a place as any for an armory." Boomer hustled off and started directing people.

"Big? I want to be turned around by morning. It'll probably take us three days, if we can even move that tank through the mountains, to the city."

Big nodded and kept his mouth shut, even though it looked like he had something he wanted to say. Some of the crowd started to shift closer.

"And, Big, this isn't conscription, so no one comes with us unless they want to, and I wouldn't mind if we tried to convince some women to stay. I well know a woman can be better than a man in lots of situations, but enough of the world has died already." He quickly glanced around. People had leaned close to hear his conversation with Big.

He cleared his throat. "It's the women who will build our future, if we're to have one."

"I hear you, Tex. I believe you. We all do." Big gestured to include the fifty or more people lining the street. A few stepped closer. Will felt that these people needed to know what they were all up against.

He spoke with caution. "It's not just men or women we are fighting... it's their misdirected beliefs and skewed morals... and the Infected they've kept alive, the Infected they're using to hunt and kill."

This was news to many of the crowd, but instead of it frightening them, he could actually see determination etch further across their faces. They eyed One Ear, who was still tied, with so much intensity that he squirmed as far away as he could get within the confines of the truck bed.

He knew he'd just been sleepwalking since after the virus, but now he wondered: had he ever really been living true, even before? He also knew he had an obligation to Rhiannon and Snickers, and to himself, to step up. The time for doubt and self-indulgence had passed. He really hoped more people wouldn't have to die; he'd always considered life precious, but enemies never seemed to play by the same rules.

He pitched his voice low. "It is in times like these that we must live the moral good, that we must strive to do so even amongst evil. But when others confuse our kindness for weakness, when others steal, rape, and murder? We must stand, and we will exact punishment."

They cheered at that, louder and more fervent than any football crowd for any of his game-winning touchdowns.

And then he knew he was right.

THEY DIDN'T DRAG HER ANYMORE, AND SHE noticed more of them, including the doctor, watching her. It wasn't an improvement over the ignoring. Plus, she'd be happier to retain her almost inhuman untouchable status. That was something she was accustomed to, something she could handle.

She lost track of time in the tunnels. They forced food on her twice, but she refused to sleep not knowing where Snickers was and when she might see the girl again.

They eventually exited into daylight and crammed into bullet-punctured trucks. She succumbed to exhaustion while they drove and lost a few more hours. She only awoke when the ride turned rocky as they plunged, insanely, into the literal bowels of the city.

Even before, this area must have been hell personified for its residents. *Why squat here when this picturesque coastal city was mostly empty?*

They crisscrossed through the streets and alleys, as if evading a tail they didn't seem to have, and finally drove right into a slum motel.

The other cars took off while they — her, the doctor, and Shriller in the back, with Grunt driving and Mandy yammering — parked in the lobby.

As they got out of the car, five others climbed in and backed out. Decoys, she guessed and almost laughed at their cloak-and-dagger play.

Brick, wood, and glass littered the lobby, like they'd just rammed a car through the front and left it a ruin. That said a lot about them, none of it good.

They crossed through the hotel out into the back alley, so that wasn't their home base. Finally, they ended up in a waterfront warehouse. Rhiannon figured the warehouse wasn't their base of operations either, but she wasn't sure if it was the lights, makeup, or wigs that gave it away.

Perhaps it was just the life-sized reproduction of her latest *Vanity Fair* cover hanging from the rafters that was the most obvious tell.

Why haul a generator to some printing house just to print that jumbo photo? She sensed she wasn't going to be able to figure these people.

There had to be twenty dresses, all in shades of green matching the one she'd worn in the cover shoot, hanging on portable racks nearby.

"After we knew he wanted you, we thought about using a double," Mandy explained as she crossed to turn on the lights ringing the mirrors. "I've been styling wigs and collecting dresses, we discarded a few ultimately unsuitable candidates... no worries, now we have the real deal." Mandy actually smiled, like Rhiannon should be excited to be included in their madness, but she'd never been a fan of spy films, too many twists.

Mandy returned to examine her in the bright light and chided, "You've lost weight you couldn't afford to lose."

"You haven't," Rhiannon smirked.

Mandy just ignored her as she turned to complain to Grunt. "This is going to take me hours. Just look at her hair: sun-bleached straw! And don't even get me started on her skin. I'm worried these are more than dehydration lines, and the uneven tan... I'll have to airbrush."

"You never did like the natural beauty look, did you, Mandy? I guess such a thing just isn't doable when you don't have the right canvas."

They'd reverted to ignoring her. Grunt, so typically, grunted in response to Mandy's bitching, then turned to settle into a dilapidated couch out of place and era against a cement wall.

"She's going to have scrapes and bruises, especially on her ribs," the doctor warned.

"I don't give a shit about her ribs. By the time he sees her ribs, it'll be too late, in more than one way." Mandy sneered with narrowed eyes in a feeble attempt to menace.

"Sleepy, Mandy?" Rhiannon asked. "Maybe you need to pee pee? Or maybe it's an infection? Get the doctor to look; wouldn't want to lose an eye."

"I hate you, Rhiannon Wells. I always did. You never, never... you're so... cold," Mandy sputtered. "I never got, never understood why —"

"Why what? Why people want to fuck me? Be me? A character on the big screen? Why not? Wasn't it better than their lives, than your life?"

Mandy stepped close, ready to hurt, ready to kill, but without the wherewithal or skill to pull it off. She was too short to be threatening. *That's what hate really looks like*, Rhiannon mused. *Guess I never really got that.* Then Grunt grunted and a little muscle went out of Mandy.

The doctor redirected the boring catfight. "The dress

has a very low back, too low to hide the rib bruising. It might spoil the package." Though she seethed at being referred to as a package, it wasn't the first time she'd been called dirty names. She opted to sow more discord.

"Actually, it has to be glued into place," she unhelpfully offered. "If you've found the right one."

"I found the right one!" Mandy snapped, and then turned on the doctor. "And I'll cover any bruises. It might take hours, but I'll make her look like the picture. I am that good." Nothing to dispute there; unfortunately, Mandy was that good, and Rhiannon Wells would be looking like her old airbrushed self in no time.

The doctor retreated to the couch, but chose to stand at the grimy window rather than sit. More red-painted freaks snuck in to get a look.

"Get her clean and into a robe. The hair will need toner," Mandy ordered Shriller, and then flounced off to play with her warpaint collection.

"I am not undressing for you," Rhiannon stated firmly.

Shriller laughed. "Oh, honey, I've seen it all!"

"Not me, you haven't," she retorted.

Mandy's giggle hit more than one false note. "Really, Rhiannon, the whole world saw those pictures. It's the Internet."

She didn't respond. She'd never done nude. There had been too many other abuses, mostly as a child, where she hadn't had a choice, so this she had rabidly protected. Thinking about it now, she wouldn't have put it past Manic Mandy to have posted those Photoshopped pictures to the Internet. *What a bitch!* As head of makeup, Mandy made at least a thousand dollars a day off Rhiannon Wells's box-office appeal. But then, she was just that good. And

Rhiannon Wells had never been one to deny anyone their talent.

"So let me get this: you're going to dress me up like that ..." — she gestured toward the life-sized *Vanity Fair* cover — "... and what, use me as bait?"

"You always were quick, Rhiannon," Mandy maliciously purred. "Don't worry; we'll give you a little script to follow along and everything."

"I understand the guy is bad news —" she started to negotiate, but Mandy flew into a rage.

"Bad news! Do you even know what he's doing?"

"Okay, Mandy, you don't have to foam at the mouth about it! I saw the baby mills. And they did slaughter everyone in my group except me."

"You always were undeservedly lucky, Rhiannon," Mandy bitched. "Your face gets you everything."

"It was my ovaries that time," she countered.

"Well, this time, it'll be us trading your face, and you'll finally do some good instead of just milking money from masturbating losers. And the fact that it will be the last moments of your life makes it an even sweeter victory." Mandy flounced her hair again and turned to open another box.

"Ouch, nasty. Have you been reading again? That's a lot of story for such a little head." Rhiannon smiled like she meant it as a compliment.

Mandy didn't rise; playtime was over. Now she was going to have to face what they wanted and figure out a way to get Snickers and get gone.

Shriller tugged her elbow toward a dressing area. "Come on, sugar," he prompted.

"And if I say no?" she tested.

Shriller shook his head. "There's no 'no' here, you get

it? You're not worth much more than that cutout to them," he cautioned. "Except you they can get in the door."

"That's what I thought." She sighed.

"They got you out the first time," he whispered. "And you weren't supposed to go back for the dog."

"That was them?" Rhiannon was surprised.

"Yep," Shriller continued, "but the dog was bait. You ruined that. Then they figured out who you were."

"Bait?" she queried casually, aware that at any moment he was going to stop answering questions.

"He collects things," Shriller answered.

"And when he collects me?" But she already knew the answer. She saw it flashing within Shriller's fervent eyes. They all watched her too closely.

Fanatics suck balls.

"Then we'll know where to find him and end his reign of terror." Shriller's eyes gleamed, and his voice took on a preacher's resonance.

"You guys aren't much better, are you? Look how you've treated Snickers and me, like meat."

Shriller physically recoiled at her suggestion. "We're saviors of the world!" he yelled. Grunt looked up from his magazine. "You are the vessel of that salvation; you should be euphoric!" Shriller continued to shrill.

"I am not, nor will I ever be, interested in sacrificing myself for your cause." She turned to face Grunt as he slowly shifted off the couch. "Give me Snickers and a gun," she offered. "I'll take care of the guy. Maybe you think I should've before, but it wasn't my place to do so."

"No," Grunt bluntly answered. "You'll do it our way. We've worked out all the angles. We know this one'll work. Take. Off. Your. Clothes."

Mandy, who was playing at styling a wig, looked up,

eager for another match of wills, ready to gobble up any energy, negative or otherwise.

The virus now tallied survivors' souls in its body count.

Rhiannon didn't know how much to gamble on them not hurting her. It wasn't just her life she was throwing away. She had Snickers to consider. They might be all half-dead inside, and though she'd known that feeling, it wasn't her anymore, not with Will and Snickers on the horizon.

"Give me Snickers. I'll do anything." She actually lifted her chin for emphasis as she counter offered. "No Snickers, no cooperative play."

The doctor sighed and rubbed his face like he didn't want to see what was to come. She had a sinking feeling she'd overplayed her hand.

Grunt lunged to grab her arm and drag her toward a desk chair that was set up in front of a TV. So they'd been ready for her refusal.

He slammed her into the chair. He slapped on the TV. She thought about attacking him, but was sure the others wouldn't let her get in many hits. The TV displayed a live feed of a street that looked to be in the middle of the city. She wondered how they'd gotten the technology working.

"Release the girl." Grunt, his hand clamped to her shoulder, spoke into a walkie. Her heart sank so heavy she couldn't breathe for a moment.

A man on the TV suddenly darted out into the middle of the street. He was carrying a little hooded person, carrying a hooded Snickers.

Rhiannon just sat there, frozen in her terror for the child as the man placed Snickers down on the double yellow, yanked off her hood, and ran. He left her there, alone and bewildered. Her arms were tied at her back, and with her broken arm, that had to hurt terribly.

Snickers, absorbing her new environment, rotated in a slow circle. In doing so, she momentarily faced the camera.

Rhiannon felt the pain of Snickers's abandonment like a knife through her heart. Mandy leaned in to whisper in her ear.

"Your fault, isn't it?"

The camera zoomed in on the sign around Snickers's neck, which read "Ask me how I know Rhiannon Wells." Her face was streaked with dirt, not tears. Snickers tried to run to the side of the street, but stumbled over her cobbled legs. She fell to her knees and, head bowed, stayed down.

Rhiannon moaned. She couldn't help it.

"Ah, Rhiannon, don't worry. Because of that sign, they'll pick up the girl and maybe take her to him. We can't track her, 'cause they'll search too thoroughly. But you, when you go in after her, he won't let anyone lay a hand on you." Mandy stroked her hair and cooed, "I've got you figured out, Rhiannon. You have a soft spot for this child; who knows why, but we'll use it."

She had her hands around Mandy's neck before anyone reacted to her move. She slammed the makeup artist to the floor and began to choke death from her. Grunt tried to yank her off, but she wasn't going anywhere until the bitch was dead. She had made a pact with Snickers, and she would honor it.

She heard the doctor yell, "Don't hurt her! Otherwise all this will be for nothing!"

Mandy's face was turning a lovely shade of purple.

She felt the sting of the needle and lost her grip on Mandy when she reached to pull it out, but in the end, the doctor was too fast.

Suddenly her ribs didn't hurt anymore.

She couldn't operate her hands.

Mandy, coughing up a lung, rolled away.

Rhiannon's eyes and then brain fogged.

She clung to her final image of Snickers abandoned on the street; that way, when she woke up, she'd remember exactly what she had to do.

She noticed they didn't let her hit the ground when she finally gave in and slumped forward.

IN THE END, ONE EAR DID ACTUALLY DRAW THEM A map. Surrounded by candles in the lounge of the hotel, they all hunched over to study it.

One Ear had obviously spent some time in art class as a kid, and took well to the crayons they'd provided; he used color liberally. The known population — blue for the bad guys, red for the other bad guys (who took Rhiannon and Snickers), and yellow for unknowns — seemed grouped around one main street. Heavily armed, barricaded checkpoints stood at the four main entry points to the city, and only one of them had a working gate.

That was, if they could trust One Ear, which Will for one certainly didn't, not for a moment.

Rhiannon must have slipped through an unclaimed part of the city to get out, but they certainly weren't getting a tank in that way.

"It's all about offensive and defensive lines," he murmured out loud, and resisted cradling his head in his hands out of hopelessness.

One Ear snorted and Big cuffed him on the back of the

head. "Let the man talk it out. You never planned to invade a city either."

Will's head shot up as he figured through Big's unwittingly accurate statement. One Ear avoided his gaze as he added details to the map.

"You guys didn't need to invade. The city was just sitting there waiting for anybody to lay claim. Hell, it would have been chaos back then, what, eight, nine months ago?"

Big nodded in agreement. One Ear was coloring in what looked like a large park surrounded by water with a large bridge spanning off it.

"No city has a park that big right in prime real estate," Big bitched. "He's lying to us, Tex. Let me remind him how to draw straight."

"It's there, Big. I saw it once, I was in town for a charity thing." Will smiled at Big's disbelief and wondered at his ability to do so in this dark hour. Except it didn't really feel that dark. He knew Rhiannon would do anything to keep Snickers safe. Hell, she threw herself off a damn cliff. So it was just Rhiannon's safety he had to worry about, and if they all were right about her being a prized possession, then he had leeway. Well, until she pissed the highest bidder off enough for them to think about doing damage in order to control her.

He forced himself to continue with the plan. "Who knows how many of the city's original inhabitants survived the virus, or stayed after."

"What's that?" Big peered at the map. "A mermaid?"

"A lady diver on a rock," One Ear clarified. "I liked watching the waves break over —"

"Why the hell would we need to know about a lady diver carved on a rock in the ocean by a park? We're planning an invasion!" Big roared.

Luanne came running from the kitchen, but her concern turned to tea-towel-wringing frustration when she saw that nothing was actually wrong.

"Big, how do you expect the man to plan, with your hollering in his ear like a lion with a sliver in his paw? Now you hush, you hear?"

A slow, easy grin spread across Big's face. "I like when you holler at me, Luanne." He mock lunged at her and she squealed in delight.

"Now don't you bother me, Big. I'm getting you boys some food. Brains need fuel for planning." She sashayed back into the kitchen.

Will wondered how a woman could change a man, but then he guessed that this Big had just been waiting under the surface for Luanne to find. Just like he'd been waiting for Rhiannon, not even knowing that she existed. Well, truthfully, not knowing that she existed in his world.

"There's no army base in or near that city; no reason for it to have been there. Which means a tank trumps anything they can counter with."

"They've got guns." One Ear's voice had taken on a whiney quality.

"Antitank?" Will quietly asked. One Ear didn't have to answer.

"There's other people too, Tex," Big cautioned as he tapped the yellow on the map. "Good people that'll just get hurt if we go in blazing."

"I know, Big, but a strong offensive will get us in the zone. And once we're in, we won't be going anywhere, plus One Ear will steer us right." He caught One Ear's eye and didn't look away until he nodded in agreement. Then he leaned back and shared a look with Big, who sighed.

"It's a shame, losing more lives. You'd think we'd have

learned our lesson when we got our asses kicked by this plague," Big mused.

"Well, I figure we couldn't fight it, or we didn't have enough time to figure out how to fight it before too many of us had died," Will said.

"Or that's the way they wanted it," One Ear mumbled, and when they turned their attention to him, he stated firmly, "The government, you know."

Big laughed. "The jokes on them, 'cause they're all dead!"

"Maybe." One Ear was back to the mumbling. "Maybe they're in a special bunker."

"First, we got to get the tank through the mountains." Will had no opinion about any government conspiracy, so he called them back to the plan.

"We could barge it downriver," Big offered.

"The same river that Snickers and Rhiannon dove in? I don't think so," he countered. "No, it's been years since I drove them, but the tunnels must be all four lane by now, hey, One Ear?"

One Ear just shrugged.

Big lifted his hand to cuff him again, but Will stopped him with, "Don't matter, that's the only way to go. No choice makes the choice easy."

"What about the cars, Tex? There'll be cars blocking the road," Big reminded him.

"Don't worry, Big. I got that covered."

As they watched One Ear with his crayons, he pondered that this was the same man who'd sworn vengeance on Rhiannon for his brother's death. Then he forced himself to remember that this was that same man, and that One Ear was never getting anywhere near Rhiannon or Snickers again. Big caught his eye and, looking almost proud, nodded again in agreement. This pact was certainly going to be hell on his mortal soul.

"I know you got it covered, Tex." Big's gruffness didn't match his soft tone. "We all trust you; even he trusts you." Big indicated One Ear.

"As long as you all know I'm no hero, and I'm not aiming to be a martyr either." He sighed. "I'm just a man doing what he sees as right."

"That's what we all like about you, Tex." Big grinned. "We don't need no savior, other than the one God himself provided; that's just fine."

"Amen," Luanne added as she, followed by a pregnant woman, carried in trays of steaming bowls and what looked like fresh bread. When Will looked up to praise Luanne's cooking, she brushed him off with a pleased smile. "Just veggies, a family recipe, nothing to it."

The pregnant woman knelt down beside him and placed a napkin on his lap. Then she picked up his bowl and offered it with downcast eyes.

B.B. growled a warning. He'd forgotten she was lounging by the fire, but obviously she hadn't been sleeping. The woman offered him a spoonful of stew. When he looked up questioningly, Big threw a look at Luanne.

"Never you mind, Emily! He's gonna look after us all," Luanne chided. She hustled around to take the bowl away from Emily and urge her to her feet; the pregnancy hampered her movements.

"But... but the baby," Emily pleaded.

"He sees you're pregnant," Luanne clucked. "He values life, but he's got a woman. I know you've been listening." She herded Emily out. B.B. settled as soon as the women cleared, but Will wondered whether she'd been protecting him or Rhiannon's territory.

"Sorry about that, Tex," Big offered. "We... well, Luanne, rescued her 'bout a month back. The father died in the last wave of the virus. The ones keeping her debated making her miscarry to see if she'd hold their seed instead, so Luanne decided it was time to part company with them."

"And now she's looking for a protector?" Will filled in the blanks.

Big shook his head. "I ain't seen her do that with anyone else."

He thought for a while as they all ate a few tasty mouthfuls. Then he said, "This is what it's come to... that a woman thinks she has to..."

He couldn't continue the thought.

Big clasped his shoulder, and even One Ear stopped coloring.

He found he couldn't continue eating either.

"Well." He cleared his throat. "We aren't so far away from equal rights and privileges that we can't get back what we've misplaced."

"It's a plan." Big slapped him on the back and then returned to scarfing stew.

"Jesus, you're going to get us all killed," One Ear moaned.

"Nah, that was the original point of sending your buddy ahead. They'll already know from where and why we're coming; we'll just finish them in the when."

WAKING WAS LIKE SWIMMING THROUGH STICKY cotton balls, but the second she surfaced, the image of Snickers on the street seared her brain. Rhiannon dampened the instinct to simply lunge off the bed or couch or whatever she was currently lying on, to take inventory. No voices; maybe she wasn't awake enough to actually hear. She felt — lighter — and it wasn't just residual from the drugs. *Her hair felt fluffy and her skin tingled... the assholes had fucking waxed her!*

A shadow loomed, and she almost flinched when something brushed against her upper lip... *Lipstick, they are making me up, unconscious or not.*

When she caught the pungent floral scent, she forced her hand into a fist; it preferred to remain lax, but her brain was raring to go. She flung her arm, fist attached, upward and was surprised at how much force she actually commanded.

Bone crunched tooth, and she opened her eyes to catch sight of Mandy clutching her bloodied mouth and reeling backwards away from the couch.

Before she could force her body to follow up the punch with an attack, the cold steel touch she'd expected against her head happened.

Audio kicked in. Mandy tried to sob through her previously injured larynx. At that hoarse sound, Rhiannon felt smugness stretch across her face.

"Dogs learn lessons quicker than you, Mandy. You. Don't. Touch. Me. Ever." Though the gun dug into her temple, she didn't lose her sneer.

She turned just enough to see Grunt on the other end of the gun. "I could kill her," she said, "and you wouldn't hurt me for fear of ruining your plans." She made sure to add Will's slow drawl to her accent to emphasize her calmness. It always seemed to work wonders for him, at least on her.

Grunt, true asshole, actually thought about it for a moment, eye-locked with Mandy, who didn't seem to like what she was seeing on his face. Then he grunted and lowered the gun. "Still, I wouldn't like it," he finally responded, and angled his body away from Mandy's betrayed look.

So she let it go, figuring the pain of Grunt's disloyalty, coupled with the neck, nose, and lip wounds, never mind Snickers's bite, was enough to keep Mandy in place for a while.

Feeling them sting, she looked down at her knuckles to see she'd cut them on Mandy's teeth. She should have forced her eyes open before she swung.

"You'll want to see this," Grunt said.

She pulled her gaze from Mandy, who hadn't yet transitioned her wounded face to her angry one, but she really, truly doubted she was interested in anything Grunt had to show. But despite winning the last battle, she knew she didn't have a say.

The doctor was tending Mandy's split lip, so he'd be able to stall any surprise attacks from that front. Mandy's front tooth looked a little loose, and Rhiannon seriously hoped the bitch lost it. That wasn't even one percent of the payback she planned to exact. Right now, Mandy was radiating wounded-animal vibes, and you always kept eye contact in that situation, though maybe she had that backward.

Grunt switched on the TV and turned it in her direction. She didn't want to see any more video, but was also desperate to see Snickers. She tightened her silk — *fucking typical* — robe. The fabric whispered across her skin to let her know she wasn't wearing anything underneath. She stretched her legs out and didn't stand until she was sure she'd be steady. She was, as always, unwilling to project a diminished image.

Grunt didn't bother waiting or watching her as he cued the video, if it was actual video; she didn't get how they got the technology to work. Actually, the only thing waiting on her was the green dress that still hung to one side. She had a feeling it wouldn't be waiting long.

Grunt blocked the screen, so she couldn't quite see what he was rewinding, but she at least knew it wasn't a live feed.

How long had she been knocked out of the game? *How long had Snickers been abandoned in the vermin-ridden streets of some goddamned city?* And by vermin, she didn't mean rats. No, she meant the rabid creatures to which humanity, without society or even religion, had devolved.

Grunt moved to give her a view of the turn her immediate future was about to take: Snickers still kneeling, on screen, wasn't alone anymore. A crowd had gathered to stare at the child, but no one approached closer than a few feet. Snickers, her hands still tied, kept her head bowed.

Rhiannon's heart ached as she watched the screen, but as two men stepped forward to claim Snickers, a slow burn spread across her chest. She recognized Buddy, Asshole's pal (One Ear according to Will), and figured that meant Asshole was nearby. So they'd gotten away from Will.

Or Will let them go, or they had Will, or they'd killed Will, or Will wasn't coming at all. She forced her focus to the TV.

She didn't know the guy with Buddy, but despite his inbred-hick appearance, he got props for untying Snickers's hands. He looked stupid but not mean.

Snickers tried to fight but could barely move her blood-deprived limbs; then, after Stupid whispered in her ear, she collapsed in his arms.

Buddy seemed to be nervous about the crowd, but they just silently watched the two men load the child into a Jeep and drive away.

Rhiannon stood and crossed to the green dress. Aware of everyone's eyes on her, she slipped her prettily French-manicured toes into the strappy gold high heels. She dropped the robe, not giving a moment's thought to standing before them naked, and slipped the dress over her perfectly curled hair. She turned to lock eyes with Grunt.

Shriller, not so shrill now, murmured, "We have to take it in more."

Mandy shushed him harshly.

Rhiannon smiled, that smile that they — the directors, the producers, and the fans — paid twenty million for, just to see her in some romantic comedy.

Grunt stumbled back from the wattage in that smile.

His eyes gooed like men's — and some women's — did when they thought they might fuck her. She deliberately used the term fuck in place of love, and she always had, but she might reconsider if she ever saw Will again.

"You'll take me to that exact spot where you left Snickers," she wooed them even while she commanded.

"We will," Mandy confirm-croaked.

"I'll be your Trojan Horse, but once I get my hands on Snickers, you better hope I never lay eyes on you again, never ever again, because —" She dropped the smile.

Grunt, the doctor, and Shriller actually slumped at the loss of it. Mandy had her arms crossed and her glare perfected.

"Not because I'll kill you," Rhiannon cooed. "I'll just stake you, bleed you, rip out your intestines and leave you ..." — she whispered now — "... for them, the Infected. If they're smart, and despite their zombieness, I believe they are smart about such things, they'll keep you alive while they eat you. And that will be good enough for me."

She smiled again, not for them, but to make sure it still worked. It was the only weapon she had now.

NO MATTER HOW MUCH HE PLANNED, ORDERED, and packed, he couldn't shake the image of Snickers slung like some sack over the ape guy's shoulder.

They — the Red Jackets as One Ear called them — had encircled but not touched Rhiannon on the riverbank. They had let her wave to him. They followed, not pushed. However, he didn't like — even the little he'd seen — their attitude toward Snickers. The girl had looked like a tool for luring Rhiannon. She'd looked disposable. So he asked One Ear and really didn't like the offhand shrug he got in response.

"The movie star is bait for the Boss," One Ear repeated.

"I got that the first time you told me." Will heard the growl in his voice; it was pretty permanent these days, but still, he didn't like it. He always figured losing your temper, yelling, throwing things and punching people meant you lost a bit of your power as well. Not that he'd never punched anyone. He just preferred to be coolheaded, so he knew he could think himself out of — not just into — a situation. Course, now the more he thought, the deeper he got.

He'd mistakenly thought he could ignore the disintegration of society. Go it alone. Then from the moment he laid eyes, he didn't need to share blood or vows with the girls to know he'd die — hell, even kill — to see them safe. He didn't take the thought of killing lightly; wasn't like he'd forgotten who he was, like so many seemed to since 99.9 percent of the world died. He'd been raised by the Ten Commandments; you didn't need to be Christian to know it was a good set of rules to live by. Seven out of ten at least.

It was pretty damn obvious people paid no heed to those rules now, but with Snickers just a child, he thought she'd be precious to all. He'd maybe seen a dozen children, including the boy in Big's group, since the plague, and he'd pretty much traveled all of North America.

Sure, some places he'd passed, he knew there were people. The ability to feel the sight of a rifle was pure instinct now. These Uncounted, who were too scared or just content alone, didn't offer tea or join the group as it passed, but they were few and far apart. Most people ran out the moment they figured they'd found a safe haven. The few groups he'd followed weren't killers, at least not indiscriminately.

Humans were social animals; at least that was what the leader of the second-to-last group had said to him the day he'd parted ways with them. But being a nomad didn't suit him. He wanted roots. He wanted to grow them himself.

He hadn't counted on needing, wanting people too. Though obviously, Snickers and Rhiannon weren't just any people. He hadn't felt compelled to go to war for anyone else, not even himself. Course, now that he thought about it, these tiny groups of Uncounted might have had something to protect, like he had Snickers and Rhiannon. Just like he'd turned away Big's group that night and would have rebuffed anyone who jeopardized him carving out a peaceful life with his girls.

He watched One Ear light another cigarette as the tense silence stretched between them. One Ear never talked unless prodded anymore. Will never did like doing all the talking, but he needed to know what to expect, what they were walking into, and One Ear was his only source.

As if absentminded, he touched the gun on his leg — he wore it strapped there like Rhiannon— and One Ear's eyes darted to follow his gesture.

Farther up the road, the guys, Dale at the wheel, winched a car on the tow truck. He'd only cleared a few miles in this direction beforehand, but now the tank needed space, both lanes, so the tow truck drove point. They also had trucks, five in total, heaped with more guns than he'd ever seen in his life, even counting action films. Among the guns, they also carried cans of gas and diesel. He didn't want to stop and siphon fuel if he could help it.

One Ear ground out his unfinished cigarette and lit another.

"Will they kill her, then, if she's of no use?" Will finally just asked One Ear outright.

One Ear watched him out of the corner of his eye and seemed to be calculating his response. He nervously flicked the cigarette away. "Nah... no point. They'd have a hard time controlling the bait if they did, wouldn't they? And the Boss will take her as bait, that he will, but on his own terms, whatever they'll be."

"Alive, then?" Will double-checked.

"And kicking," One Ear snorted, but not in an amused way. "He always likes them alive, to begin at least."

He got that One Ear was trying to needle him, but still couldn't help bristling at the threat.

"Until what?" he growled. "He likes them alive until?"

"Till they don't give him what he wants; till they don't spark, as he calls it. He's repopulating the world, just him, just his seed. Except..." One Ear trailed off and fumbled with his cigarette pack, which being empty, didn't offer any distraction. Before this, One Ear had never spoken against his boss.

"Except..." Will prompted, getting a bit fed up. Conversation should be easy, though this was more of a constant interrogation, he supposed.

"Except," One Ear continued, "except no one ever has, with him. There, ah... some of the others have... have contributed without him knowing... to save specific women, 'cause once they're knocked up, he ignores 'em, but it's risky. Men have died for it."

"He kills all the women he can't impregnate?" Will didn't really need clarification, but asked for it anyway.

One Ear nodded an affirmation.

"And he has never successfully impregnated any woman?"

Again, though he couldn't maintain eye contact, One Ear nodded confirmation.

"How many women has he... has he killed? How many women have you captured and allowed him to kill?"

One Ear responded with that shrug again.

He was beginning to really loathe shrugs. *What kind of answer was a shrug, anyway? What the hell did it even mean?*

One Ear stumbled back from what he saw grimaced across Will's face.

"He... he... she... she... she's a prize, he won't kill her," One Ear stuttered.

"What about all the other women?" Will was roaring, and nothing about yelling made him feel like he was losing any power over the situation. One Ear actually cowered at the side of the road.

The constant beeping of the tow truck was overridden by the blood rush in his ears. He rode the rage of his frustration: his inability to fix all, to move this ragtag army at pace and, always nagging, his fear for the girls. Tension ripped across his face. He glared at this cowering pile of weakness before him, this soulless piece of dirt, a man by dick only. A man who barely deserved the oxygen he stripped from the atmosphere, oxygen he poisoned just by breathing —

The crunch of gravel announced Big's presence. In fact, all work clearing the road seemed to have stopped to watch him with One Ear.

He was pleased to note he hadn't pulled his gun, and when he looked from One Ear to Big's grinning face, he felt he'd passed some test. He wasn't some rabid killer; he wasn't changing into the man he felt haunting his every choice. He'd do what was needed, but not needlessly.

Big gave One Ear a nudge with the toe of his boot. One Ear, in his unbalanced cower, tipped right over and took the tension with his fall.

B.B., who never left Will's side these days as if afraid of losing him too, pounced on One Ear, ready to tear his throat out, but playfully.

"We need to move faster, Big," Will complained, not for the first time. But Big, as always, was patient on this point.

"I know, Tex. I know."

One Ear twisted away from B.B., whose growl rippled

like laughter. He scrambled to right his dignity, of which there wasn't much to regain.

Rav, one of the many men with them on this strike, who liked to wear multiple ties, lured One Ear away with a fresh pack of cigarettes.

"It's my turn in the tow truck," Will offered as terse explanation before he headed off without waiting for Big. "We'll be at the tunnel tomorrow if we work straight through."

They all had, in fact, worked in shifts every day since he'd lost the girls. He found he could get by on two hours' sleep no problem. He hadn't heard one complaint, and not just because they treated him with deference, but also because they wanted something they could fight. They'd lost to the plague without even attempting to mount a defense; at least he didn't know if the governments ever managed any. They'd lost wives, children, everyone. You couldn't shield a loved one from a virus, or pummel it with your fists, or even reason with it.

It wasn't natural for a man to just sit and let trouble stride through his door. A man needed to be in action; otherwise, he wasn't a man.

The world had measured him by how far he could throw a ball, or run, or degrees he could get, but now he wielded a different ruler. And anyone who didn't measure up wasn't going to make the cut. That wasn't just his decision; they were unanimous in their support.

If order was achieved through dictatorship in this world, it was going to be his for a while; and thank God, he now knew he'd be benevolent.

SHE CHECKED HER REFLECTION IN COMPARISON TO the cover shot in the mirror.

"Mandy," she snapped, "this lipstick isn't the right shade!" Mandy double tripped in her effort to cross to her side.

"I... I... It was the nearest match I could find."

"Mix something," she demanded. "I thought you said he'd only accept his ideal of me?" She had her signature sneer back in place.

"Y-yes, y-you heard right." Mandy butterfingered the lipstick tubes.

She locked eyes with Grunt in the mirror; he hadn't stopped staring since she put on the dress.

"If you're going to force me to do this... I'll do it my way... as close to perfection as I can get. Snickers doesn't need any amateur effort." Rhiannon directed that last sneer at Mandy. She felt back in charge and on solid ground. Well, as solid as one could feel in a room full of people who were about to sacrifice you.

She could see the thoughts flitting across their faces,

especially the doctor's: better her than me, than my mother or daughter or... but the big flaw in that logic was that no one had mothers or daughters to defend anymore, so what made her and Snickers so easily sacrificial?

Yes, women were being exploited here, so save them, heal them, get out of town — the world was a big empty place — take over your own city.

Anyway, it was stupid of her to spend any brain matter on untangling their logic. Rational reasoning wasn't high on their to-do list.

"You'll take me to the place we last saw Snickers," she demanded again.

"We already said that, Rhiannon." Mandy was getting testy.

"I'm ready now." She turned to stride to the door. Grunt woke out of his staring stupor.

"Wait, tracking devices." Grunt nodded to Shriller.

"You... you don't even know where to find this Boss guy?" Rhiannon's belly bottomed. Snickers was on the block and they hadn't even figured out their entry plan.

"Told you, nobody ever sees him except his inner circle," Mandy reminded her. "And he doesn't give a shit about them, no matter how many we kill."

"Yeah, you didn't actually mention that, Mandy. How do you even know he exists, then?" Rhiannon didn't fancy dying or losing Snickers for nothing.

"People talk." Mandy shrugged and tested a shade of lipstick.

Shriller kept trying to slip his hand and some device up Rhiannon's skirt. She batted him away.

"Not there," she snapped. "If he's the romantic you make him out as, the garter is the first thing he'll go for, with his teeth, probably."

Shriller looked to Grunt, who seemed to be thinking; it looked like hard work for him, so she turned to Mandy for more answers.

"Talk doesn't make a person real," she prompted.

"No?" Mandy retorted sweetly, with a raised eyebrow. Good point. Celebrity was all talk.

"Sew it in the dress," Grunt finally offered.

"No! No! You'll ruin it." Mandy practically shrieked, causing Shriller to back off.

Who the fuck was in charge here? Rhiannon didn't like being trapped in some power struggle, ever — same as not mucking in the middle of a marriage.

"She's got to have more than one on her, Mandy." Grunt was running out of patience for all this girly shit.

"But, Dean, babe," Mandy cooed. "On this dress it'll stand out like a lump, anywhere. What about her shoe, can you tape it to the bottom?" Mandy fluttered her eyelashes.

Seeing this misuse of female power made Rhiannon a bit gaggy. Some women didn't get that you chose your battles and you made them mean something. You didn't just give it away every time you opened your mouth. Men weren't that simple.

"Yeah, try the shoe." Grunt gave in.

"Fuck, watch any movies lately? They'll find it right away," Rhiannon griped. "It'll just tip them off."

"That's why you'll swallow the other one." Grunt bared his teeth in what she took to be some sort of flirty grin, like they were cohorts. She couldn't totally hide the distaste she felt at this bonding attempt, which didn't smooth anything with her and Mandy, who had hawk eyes. She tried to be pleasant, she really did — no — that was just a blatant lie.

"My stomach acid won't work well with any tracking thing —"

"We tested it." Grunt approached with an object in his pudgy fingers. She was surprised he had the motor skills to grasp something so small.

"It works for about an hour." He held the chip, or whatever the fuck it was, close to her mouth. "And you'll sure keep him occupied for a lot longer than that."

Hmmm, a threat, but not really, because he spoke the truth; but he was trying to threaten, so he'd taken exception to her distaste as well. She opened her mouth as little as possible and attempted to keep edge out of her tone.

"What if it takes longer than an hour to get to him?"

Grunt paused, his hand at the back of her neck, and looked to Mandy, whose eyes were actually glittering at seeing Rhiannon physically threatened.

Man, these people were seriously fucked up.

Then he just grunted, grabbed her jaw, and shoved his stubby sausage fingers down her throat. She would have swallowed it if asked nicely.

Afterward, she thought about throwing up on him, but she didn't have anything in her stomach to project. Mandy had to fix her lipstick.

She figured Grunt redeemed himself in Mandy's eyes with that show of brute force, and she wanted to get out of there before he got his reward.

She grabbed the clutch purse — she figured it probably held a tracking chip as well — and the shawl — for show, not warmth, and headed for the door. They seemed a little dumbfounded at her brisk movement, her willingness to get on with it, but what else was there to talk about? Or maybe they were expecting reprisal for the fingers-in-her-throat bit? She was more interested in exacting revenge after she got Snickers.

It wasn't like they were going to give her a gun, even if

she asked nicely, so she'd improvise; plus, their dynamics were just a headache.

She longed for the peacefulness of just a moment with Will, but then shook it off with a promise to herself: *Save Snickers and get Will — if —* if she could pull it off.

She pivoted at the door to look back. They gaped, of course. She might as well have been on a red carpet lit with thousands of flashes.

Action had been called.

TIME, AND HIS ENDLESS TRACKING OF IT, HAD tuned down to the step-by-step moving of the next car or truck, though not all needed to be towed.

Wedge the tow truck near the obstacle, hitch it, winch it, and move it to one side. Zero in on the next flagged vehicle, and so on, and on.

Teams led by Dale or Rav fanned out in front and went from car to car to see if they'd move on their own steam. A surprising number did. Some were empty, like the owners just abandoned them out of hopelessness, not lack of gas; but most cars were still unfortunately occupied. These corpses were dried, husk-wrapped skeletons. The plague had been all phlegm and fluid, but these victims — after death, Will supposed — had slowly baked in their cars. Many cars were filled with families, who he thought might have been on their way to a major city for medical help, and not all had died from the virus.

He wondered at a father's ability to watch his loved ones die, to stand strong as all was failing, but then be unwilling to go on alone. It wasn't a choice he'd ever been faced with, and honestly, under the circumstances of everyone else dying, life was the only thing.

It was ironically amusing that, even if he were unwilling to take his own life, he'd take another's if it meant saving Rhiannon and Snickers.

They laid the dead to the side of the road with — if they had it — a blanket or something to cover them, but they didn't have time for burials. They had discussed leaving the bodies in the cars; it wasted precious time to move them, but it didn't hurt to be respectful, even in these days.

They finally got by a sharp corner and the six-car wreck piled there, and Will could see the outline of the tunnel with the late-afternoon sun beyond. They had widened it to four lanes, and not even knowing his own doubt, he suddenly felt like this plan might actually have a chance of working.

Course, from here it was impossible to see if even two lanes was wide enough for a tank, let alone high enough for it to pass through.

Like his mom had always said — though years after her death, he realized she'd been paraphrasing Scarlett O'Hara — he'd worry tomorrow. Tonight, he'd comfort himself in the thought that the rays of the ready-to-set sun that blurred his vision also shone on Snickers and Rhiannon.

He didn't think that was overtly romantic, just a matter of weather and geographical proximity. Still, it lightened his soul.

She stepped into the street and instantly knew by the goosebumps on her arms that this was not an evening for which this dress was intended.

A city should never be this silent... buildings like jutting bones of a rotting skeleton... Suddenly claustrophobic, Rhiannon struggled to breathe. This, she quickly informed herself, was silly, and she never did think silly looked good on her; but the country — *Will's country* — had never felt this dead. A city needed people. Earth needed nothing but the elements.

She shook off these uncharacteristically deep thoughts and focused: *Snickers.*

She oriented herself and then stepped into the center of the street to where she thought might have been the very spot Snickers had knelt. She'd been hoping for some trace of the child here, but what could she manage to leave behind being gagged and bound?

She felt the clustered Red Jackets behind her and wished she could kill with a look; but she couldn't, so she didn't bother looking back.

"We're going to leave you now, Rhiannon," Mandy peeped.

"Here I was hoping you were already gone," she answered, but didn't put much weight behind it. She was conserving energy. Still, even without turning to see, she felt her words slap Mandy mute. *What did the bitch think, that they'd been bonding at gunpoint?*

She stepped forward. Her three-inch-heeled sandals didn't like the cobblestones, but she'd walked in worse. Farther along, the street was paved.

In the end, she left them behind, not the other way around.

She walked half a block, not interested in waiting for the second set of bad guys, before becoming aware of a hot, pressing energy. She wasn't particularly in tune with that sort of thing, but if enough people stared at you, you eventually felt it. These stares burned.

Then suddenly, people were just there — in the alleys, slipping out of doorways. So the city was dead despite being inhabited — *haunted*?

They wore pieced-together clothing — black, gray, brown — so that it was difficult to distinguish them from the buildings, which, she guessed, was the point. With 99.9 percent of the world dead, you'd better believe better clothing choices were available, so these were definitely uniforms of choice.

They watched her as if she were a ghost. *An apparition of the past, maybe*? Then she realized what she must look like. The green silk of her dress trailing, sun-kissed hair that framed her practically flawless face... She looked like... a... goddess — or rather — a movie star. They were following her now, slowly slipping along the edges of the buildings... and —

Was that a child who was quickly thrust from view by a protector who wouldn't meet her eye, but whose own gaze burned the second she turned away?

The street in front remained empty, and remembering the role she was to play, she stifled a growl of frustration that bubbled in her throat.

A brisk, salty wind — they must be very close to the ocean here — blew through the buildings and billowed around and beyond her. The dress was instantly slicked against her. She could feel the light fabric lift about four feet behind her, her hair setting a similar sail. Her silk-sheathed nipples rose in protest of the chill, and a murmur punctuated with gasps rustled through the following crowd. She gritted her teeth at the exposure, at the perceived sexuality, at the perceived vulnerability of an involuntary bodily function.

They reached for her then.

Lining the sides of the street suddenly as far as she could see, they reached fingers for her but didn't touch.

She walked like that for a full block, so close she could feel the brush of energy from each fingertip, thousands of fingers.

What was she to them? The time before? Whatever it was, it wasn't a role she was willing to accept or that she was even qualified for.

Having a pretty face, a sleek body, and the ability to recite lines didn't make you a god. Didn't they know what the perfect façade, which took three hours to apply, hid underneath? No, they didn't see beyond the billboard image.

Will had never mentioned her past, even when she'd left openings like conversation bombs for him to detonate. And Snickers? Snickers didn't care who she'd been, just who she was, how she protected and loved. Of all the things she would choose for herself... maybe... *mother*... she hesitated even within her own thoughts... *wife* —

Tires screeched and pulled her attention out of her ass and back to the road in front. Ah, here were the bad guys she'd been expecting.

The crowd peeled back a bit, but then waved forward as if it might swallow her rather than let her go.

Still they didn't touch her.

The machine guns, fired just over their heads, made them duck but not run. Their murmur took on an angry tone, but it was Buddy she watched.

Buddy, sans machine gun, swung down from the Jeep and crossed to her. The not-so-stupid hick hovered behind, wanting to approach but holding off the crowd.

She bared her teeth in a pseudosmile as Buddy reached for her, and he thought better of it. His hand hovered in the air by her bare shoulder.

The crowd pressed, and she suddenly realized she had an army behind her; she could take what she wanted by force. She wasn't sure what played on her face, but Buddy didn't look so happy.

"Where's your asshole friend?" Her voice was crisp in the damp air.

The crowd swelled in response to her aggression.

Stupid stepped closer, but Buddy waved him back like they'd already had a discussion.

"He didn't make it back," Buddy begrudgingly offered. She couldn't quash a real smile, and Buddy, taking exception, added, "He's not dead."

"Not yet." She narrowed her eyes so he'd see the predator behind the threat, and he did, but seemed to be deliberating over his next move.

"You'd like to hit me?" she aloofly queried.

"More than hit," he spat. "You're a package of chaos, all right, and not worth it, far as I can see."

She acknowledged his summary for the truth it held. A truth it normally took those close to her — once they were tired of fucking her — to see.

The crowd disagreed.

"You want to control your pack," Buddy ordered, referencing the crowd, but she remembered his run-in with B.B. and smiled. He handily wiped that smile off with the next threat.

"How many more people need to die for you?"

She was so done with him for now. She stepped by him, felt him stumble backwards as the crowd tried to follow, and climbed gracefully into the back seat of the Jeep.

Buddy's machine-gun goons, who she noted hadn't been present when they grabbed Snickers, slowly tightened the perimeter and jumped in cars.

Stupid quickly claimed the passenger seat and urged the driver to, "Hightail it outta here."

The driver was only too glad to take this order.

Meanwhile, Buddy was having a bit of an issue getting into the other side of the back seat without being ripped apart by the crowd. A couple of machine-gun- and goon-clad cars came to Buddy's rescue, and he pulled himself, panting, into the seat beside her. Though it was petty, his struggle amused her. She was going to pay for her smugness later, she usually did, but still she enjoyed the moment.

The crowd pressed the Jeep, and for a moment, she thought, *They aren't going to let me go.* But then the machine guns offered their opinion.

"It's a balance of power," she mused. "You can't kill them without inciting a revolt."

Buddy snorted. "They are us, lady. We're the same."

"Really? Let's see."

A few people were actually clinging to the back and sides of the Jeep. She pressed her hand against the side window.

The grubby man by her window blinked in shock and then, with a wide grin, pressed his hand to the opposite side of the glass.

"Stop that!" Buddy barked.

The Jeep lurched as the driver, following soft-spoken instructions from Stupid, tried to negotiate the crowd.

Grubby's smile spread through the crowd, and more hands were pressed around his against the glass. Their exuberance rocked the Jeep.

Rhiannon laughed and the crowd laughed with her.

"Stop, stop it!" Panic edged Buddy's demand, and then she heard him check the ammo in his gun.

Grubby croaked out a joyful hooting tune as if pied-pipering the others, who then took up his song as they kept pace with the Jeep. Through these window-pressed bodies, she caught a glimpse of the massive crowd following. She didn't know this many people were still alive. Then she saw that they too had guns and were, in fact, passing them hand-to-hand as if readying some plan.

Buddy started cursing and mumbling about an escape route and plans into a walkie-talkie.

The Jeep couldn't move any farther.

More people were about to die, all because she had a point to prove. And all she really wanted was Snickers, Will, and a warm place to sleep.

She stopped smiling.

Grubby, thrown by this abrupt change, stopped smiling.

She shook her head deliberately.

Grubby looked sad.

She waved goodbye, and Grubby reluctantly let go of the side of the Jeep.

She continued to wave; the crowd — excepting Grubby, who just looked forlorn — waved back, still following but not at such an intense pace.

"Package of chaos," Buddy muttered under his breath, but he kept his gaze firmly fixed away from her. He was still white-knuckling his gun.

"Well, that was a ride," Stupid declared, and she could hear by his accent she was right about his heritage. "At least nobody bit anybody." Stupid lobbed a laugh Buddy's way, and then she noticed the bandage on Buddy's forearm. When she looked up, she caught Stupid watching her.

"The girl's got a set of teeth, don't she?" Stupid asked. "I bet she gets that from you."

"Movie stars don't bite," Rhiannon answered archly.

Buddy snorted and then sneered. "You do what you get paid to do, like any old whore. That's all movie stars ever were, high-paid whores."

"Was I?" Rhiannon answered pleasantly enough, still watching Stupid, who was looking at Buddy like he might do him some imaginative harm.

Buddy caught this and said defensively, "Ain't no reason to speak to her. Plus, the Boss wouldn't like it." They held a manly staredown.

Then Stupid turned up front and started chatting with the driver. The Jeep had picked up so much speed that buildings were beginning to blur.

"I remind you of someone?" Rhiannon asked Buddy. "Your mother? Men are so simple sometimes. You hate the part of me that reminds you —"

"You ain't nothing like my mother, rest her soul,"

Buddy snapped. "You shut your mouth about it." Stupid looked back over his shoulder.

She didn't want to talk to him anyway; she was just distracting the nerves with garbage instead of dwelling on what was to come, except —

"The girl... just tell me if..." she stumbled to speak her fear out loud, but Stupid answered willingly enough.

"Girl's fine, you'll see soon."

"And your man?" Buddy jeered. "You don't ask about him? Don't wonder if he followed you into the river? Guess any old man will do you."

She, silently and deliciously, in a sick, sick way, added Buddy to the list of people to kill before she died.

Plus, she knew Will was all right. There wasn't any other way for it to be.

THERE WAS NO DAMN WAY THE GODDAMNED TANK was going to fit through the fucking tunnel.

Big tried suggesting another route. That all they had to do was backtrack and come through another, higher pass. Will declined.

They tried to stop him, but seeing as how they didn't seem willing to actually tackle and tie him, he continued to climb into the tank.

He'd been patient.

They cleared the oncoming lane.

They measured the tank.

They told him it wouldn't fit.

By six damned inches.

Backtracking would take, at minimum, another day. He had a bad feeling he'd lose the girls if it took him another two days to get to them.

Besides, what the hell was a tank for if not ramming its way through concrete and steel?

They shouted, arms waving, about responsibility, suicide missions, and killing them all as they ran ahead of the lurching tank. Will wasn't too smooth at the controls, but he could see the goal line; so though he might have been slow, nothing was going to stop him from getting there.

They ran through ahead to the relative safety of the other side, because there was no question he was going to take the tunnel down with this stunt. The only question was whether he'd make it through to the other side or end up a hundred feet below in the river with the tank on top of him.

He waited until the last minute to decide where he'd find that extra six inches, inside pillars or outside? It was Boomer who made up his mind.

Boomer ran ahead, not as far as the others, and more than once looked back over his shoulder with the most wicked, almost pained grin. Will's own descent into insanity was echoed in Boomer's face. He hoped, if he lived, he'd find his way back from that edge before they hit the city.

Just as the tank was about to ram through the mouth of the tunnel, Boomer reached up and patted an inner pillar as he ran by, so Will cranked right.

He half-smashed the first pillar.

The tank lost speed.

He hit the gas, death-gripped the stick to stay his course, and hit the second pillar.

He kept his eyes on the road ahead, ignoring the rather large — earth-shattering, someone more poetic might say — concrete slams behind him.

Six more pillars to go.

Course, the terrified looks on the guys, who all kept stumbling back farther and farther away from the tunnel's exit, didn't help his confidence.

Hitting pillar number three made him lose control, and suddenly, the cliff was way too close on the left.

He cranked the stick opposite.

The tank was moving like... well, like a damn tank moving through a massive vat of molasses.

He almost had the behemoth back on track when something hit the back end hard.

He'd lost momentum.

The tunnel collapse was catching up.

Will flung his entire body against the gas and stick, knowing extra weight usually didn't matter in such situations. The tank screeched.

He was pretty sure he was bleeding from his hands because his grip felt slicker than just palm sweat. He added his voice to the tank's cry. He swore. He promised blood, sacrifices, vengeance, and obedience, but he wasn't praying, not to God. He was begging the tank.

The tank, Delilah, found her feet. She grabbed, tore the

concrete below, and busted away from the weight attempting to crush her from behind.

The scream of triumph that ripped his throat did lasting damage to his vocal cords, and afterward, he always croaked when in higher octaves.

United, they lurched forward.

Gaining more momentum, they blew through pillar four, then five.

Delilah ate concrete for breakfast and lunch.

Ahead, Rav, realizing the tow truck was in the path of destruction, ran to it and jumped in. The others scattered after him.

Will was a disaster in the moment of its greatest carnage.

He realized he was laughing, a little insanely, as the tank smashed through pillar six.

A voice, not his own, cautioned this behavior; he ignored it, urged on Delilah — who was the one in control anyway — and took out pillar seven.

The exit of the tunnel was right there, maybe twenty feet away now. A little belatedly he realized they hadn't cleared enough cars. These cars — God, he hoped there were no bodies in them — actually flipped up and over the tank as Delilah slammed through them.

He hit the brakes, couldn't figure out if they worked, and in that second, couldn't decide if he preferred a river or rock death.

Delilah chose the cliff-face option, and mounted another car as she veered toward it.

He must have blacked out, because the next thing he was aware of was the blood in his eyes and the guys cheering and pounding on the tank.

Overhead, Boomer, still grinning madly, wrenched

open the hatch and reached his hand down to offer Will a lift.

He remembered to turn Delilah off.

Then he was sitting on top of the tank, which was on top of a car, which was wedged against a cliff face. He breathed the sweet summer air.

He noticed he could see through blood, that the concrete dust hadn't settled yet, and that no one else seemed to think he was insane. Though they had accused him of just that when he'd shared his plan.

He thought about smiling, so he did.

The men clapped him on the back.

There was nothing he wouldn't destroy for the girls. Course he'd never collapsed a tunnel before; that was a first, but it wouldn't be his last obstacle.

AT SOME POINT THEY BLINDFOLDED HER, LIKE IT was something they were supposed to do right away but the riled crowd threw them and they forgot. Before they put the silk tie over her eyes, she figured they were in the center of the city's business district. The use of the tie as a blindfold, which smelled strongly of men's cologne, maybe Obsession, felt overly planned and very deliberate. She felt like there was a clue in that choice, but never had been particularly good at working out puzzles. She preferred her shades of gray dark and her plotlines action oriented.

The sun was almost set. Not that that knowledge helped at all; even after fleeing it, she had no idea how the city was laid out except that it was surrounded by water. Which certainly made it harder to escape — or invade — which she imagined was the point of trying to settle here.

Why was it that megalomaniacs arose out of disaster? Maybe humans were, by nature, a herd animal and had an ingrained need to follow? But why follow insanity? Why do they not only allow themselves to be led to the edge of the cliff, but also jump off on command?

The Jeep stopped so abruptly she almost smacked her head on the seat in front of her. The car shifted, and a whoosh of air indicated her door had opened.

She turned to step out, blind. They didn't touch her more than necessary, and after she got out, they took her blindfold off in a hurry.

She was in a parking garage with every expensive car she'd ever seen in existence. In fact, this might be the sum of all expensive cars ever in the city. Wet concrete indicated that the gleaming cars had been recently washed. The fluorescent overheads worked, but waned every so often.

Buddy, Stupid, and the driver stood in an almost-huddle and stared at her. Well, Buddy wasn't actually making eye contact, unlike the others.

She pulled a pin from her hair. Grunt had made Mandy glue a tracking bug underneath the rhinestone heart. She offered the pin to Buddy.

"I'm not here to cause any chaos, any more chaos. Please, will you just take me to the girl?" She never did like pleading, but was afraid not to in this case.

Buddy took the bug with a snort and without speaking — actually none of them had spoken for a while — crushed it under his boot heel. Then he eyed her rather distastefully.

Perhaps he had a hate-on for all women?

Having made some assessment, he then said, "Follow me."

He turned toward a stairwell and Rhiannon followed, all the time knowing it wasn't going to be this easy.

Stupid brought up the rear.

A couple of sets of steel fire doors and one set of stairs later, they entered what was obviously the lobby of a five-star hotel, not a chain. Except when everyone had been dying, those five stars had meant nothing to pillagers — or rather, the survivors — so the fact that this hotel was in such pristine condition was definitely odd.

They crossed the plush carpet — her heels actually sank in — towards the bathrooms. Buddy opened the door to the women's and she frowned.

"You want me to use the washroom?" she asked as disdainfully as possible.

"I want you to throw up the bug they probably made you swallow," Buddy retorted.

She racked her brain, rapid-fire, for an excuse. "My lipstick —"

"Don't worry; he'll have that exact one, I'm sure. He expects perfection, not just from you." Buddy wasn't taking no for an answer. "You're an expert at upchucking, aren't you?" He attempted a taunt, but was too invested to make it really sting.

Of all the shit she had done, regularly regurgitating meals wasn't on her long and embarrassing — embarrassing in the face of the end of the world — list.

Damn, she really did hate throwing up and never ever

believed that it would make her feel better, even as a tummy-aching child.

"I'd be happy to stick a finger down your throat for you," Buddy threatened with a pleased smile. He gleefully anticipated this possibility.

Buddy eyed her and then followed partway as she crossed to a stall. The doors were wood; the floor and counters, marble.

"We're not stupid. We know, he knows, you're bait. Doesn't mean we're gonna get caught taking you."

Rhiannon snagged two white terrycloth towels off the counter as she passed. She placed one on the floor in front of the toilet bowl and carefully knelt. The other she draped across her chest and over her shoulders. She contemplated the toilet; it was cleaner than anything she'd seen in a while. She was going to ruin her makeup, perhaps her manicure, and seriously damage her tooth enamel.

Buddy's restless feet squeaked on the tile.

She felt petty for debating forcing herself to vomit with a chance to rescue Snickers, but she couldn't be a saint every fucking minute.

She shoved her finger down her throat, triggered her gag reflex, and threw up: water.

Fuck!

She was going to have to heave her guts again. Maybe if someone had thought to feed her. She gagged again and again, and finally the little black bug sank to the bottom of the bowl.

"Done?" Buddy prodded after only giving her a moment's breath.

She stood up and took the toothbrush kit he offered. She brushed her teeth and watched Stupid and Buddy in the mirror. They didn't speak; in fact, Stupid looked to be blocking Buddy from the exit. Not that she was interested in their drama; she just wanted Snickers and to flee, and she hoped, fiercely, that that was still a possibility.

She felt bad about spitting in the sterile sink and carefully swished any remnants away, all the while wondering when she'd gotten so... soft.

She turned to Buddy and opened her arms wide. "Anything else?"

Buddy made a sour face.

Stupid supplied the words. "Aren't supposed to search you."

She raised an eyebrow.

"Searching involves touching," Stupid elaborated.

"The Boss'll take care of that part all by himself," Buddy sneered.

Even though she was often guilty of it herself, Rhiannon decided she didn't like it when people smiled at you but meant you deep, dark damage.

"If you're done chatting, perhaps we can get on with this, then. I don't imagine your boss is the type who likes to wait." She didn't smile.

Stupid stepped away from the door. Buddy, who didn't slap her like he obviously wanted to, led the way back out into the lobby.

An older woman, dressed in a chef's uniform, scurried by the native-carved pillars and around a massive floral arrangement toward Buddy.

Where the hell had they found fresh flowers? Maybe they were silk? Nope.

"What are you doing here?" Buddy snarled at the chef's approach.

"I... I... I... the... the dinner," she stuttered and cowered, but also managed to glance numerous times at the breathtaking movie star.

"Has nothing to do with me," Buddy spit as he yelled. *He should work on breathing technique,* she thought, *though maybe he didn't mind a little extra saliva.*

"I... I... we... we... don't have any asparagus," the chef continued despite her terror, voice dropping into a whisper. "He'll... he'll kill me."

"He must have a thing for greens." Rhiannon couldn't help the sarcasm under the circumstances.

Stupid stifled a laugh.

Buddy darted dagger eyes.

The chef gaped at her like she'd just offered to suck the Pope off or something, but Buddy forcefully called her attention back.

"He's not going to give a shit what's on his plate once he has her," he bellowed.

"But, but," the chef persevered, "he wants it just like —"

"He's going to be more pissed that you delayed us, that you left the kitchen, that you laid eyes on her, isn't he?" Buddy raised his hand. The chef actually squeaked and then scurried off, presumably in the direction of the kitchen.

Buddy also took off, but towards elevators.

They didn't need to wait for an elevator; one was waiting for them. Buddy muttered about chaos as he pressed the button for the penthouse.

While the elevator ascended, she had a few moments to think.

First, she wondered — marveled — at them wasting power on an entire hotel.

Second, she thought briefly that it was going to be difficult to escape from the top of a luxury hotel with probably only one viable way down.

Third, she was happy the hotel was only fourteen floors including the penthouse, and hoped that this would be unlucky for someone other than her.

Fourth, just before the doors opened, she saw herself in the glass and realized, despite the clothing and makeup, that she was a different person.

That was something to smile about.

THERE WASN'T MUCH TO TALK ABOUT. IT WAS ALL just do and do and do. They didn't stop to camp or sleep. They ate what they had in pocket.

One Ear went without.

B.B. got extras.

The tank had been damaged, but it still moved and — Boomer thought — would still be able to fire its rounds, which was the most important thing.

He had been lucky, but no one told him so.

As the night darkened around them, they rounded the corner from which he'd been forced to watch the Red Jackets take Rhiannon and Snickers.

He didn't stop to contemplate. The city was on the horizon.

He turned to Big, who, for the moment, was off the radio and driving the truck.

"How long from here?" he asked, realizing he might not have spoken in hours.

"You didn't come this way, Tex?"

"No, I came along the Cascades, never crossed west."

"Most went west. What do you call it, what birds do?"

"Migrate?"

"Something, migration, like birds, all of us heading west after that shit ate everyone else alive. Hoping maybe that the west was virus-free, as the rumors had it in the beginning."

"Could be," he answered, but he didn't really have an opinion. He hadn't felt compelled west. "How long now, Big?" he asked again.

Big thought about it, though Will was pretty sure he knew the answer off the top of his head.

"You'll be there by dawn, Tex," Big said.

He laughed and then waited until the silence washed the harshness away.

"Dawn is not a good time to be killing people," he mumbled.

Big kept his eyes steady on the road. Will could only see the twenty or so feet the headlights illuminated.

"Nope," Big finally answered.

"Are there a lot of people in the city?" Now that he'd started asking questions, he couldn't seem to stop.

Big sighed. "Good amount, but it might not have to be that way, Tex. Killing at dawn, I mean," Big said, knowing in what direction Will's thoughts lay.

"I hope not, Big. I really do."

"But it ain't right, what they're doing to women and children, and them who stayed when they could have gone are involved."

"Complicit."

"Right."

"So even if their blood is on our hands, it'll be for the right reasons," Will said.

Big seemed very firm in this belief.

The city lights, so far and yet achingly near, hovered at the horizon beyond the swath of darkness that covered river and forest between.

They wound around another corner in their twisty descent through the valley, and Will lost sight of the beckoning lights.

"We're going to need a bullhorn," he said, a little surprised to hear he spoke the half-formed thought out loud.

"All right, then," Big answered unquestioningly, constantly supportive.

SHE WASN'T TOO SURE WHAT SHE'D BEEN expecting, but as the doors of the elevator slid open to reveal the penthouse, it sure wasn't this.

This — this room — seemed oddly familiar even though the modern furniture was completely at odds with the heritage feel of the hotel. And it was cold. Even though hotels didn't generally project a lived-in feel, they were rarely cold, as if just for display... like a film set.

Buddy stepped out of the elevator, brushed her shoulder as he passed, and surveyed the empty room. The elevator doors started to close.

Stupid angled his body around hers and shoved out an arm to stop the doors from fully closing.

Then he waited.

Buddy turned to look at her.

She sensed that even they weren't totally sure what they were leading her into, like this was foreign ground. Buddy kept looking around.

The elevator opened directly into a grand room, a living and dining combo. Double doors, closed, to the left might lead to the master suite. Steel and glass, square and mini-malist furniture dominated the decor. Even the expected traditional crown moldings were nowhere to be seen.

Buddy finally spoke. "I guess this is your playground."

She stepped from the elevator, looked around, but didn't get what he was implying.

"What? You don't recognize it? He's been working on it since you were first sighted, since before your group was brought in."

"So 'brought in' is the new lingo for murdered, is it?" Rhiannon sneered as she rotated 360 degrees to case the room. It was empty and familiar.

Buddy just shrugged and stepped to look out the window at the water view. The last stains of red sunset slowly bled from the night sky.

Stupid had settled with his back against the wall behind her, beside the elevator. She noted only one elevator door, not three like in the lobby.

She couldn't figure if Stupid was guarding her or Buddy, but it didn't really matter. It was this hanging around that bothered her now.

"So... are we waiting for a flood, a burning bush, or are we going to do each other's nails and trade hair tips?" she queried, venomless. She was all dressed up and only halfway to the ball. Her instinctual brain screamed to find Snickers while her rational side cautioned.

"We're here. Now we wait." Buddy didn't look at her when he answered.

Rhiannon remembered the last time she waited in this city, the dark room. She wondered if any of those women were still alive — sterile or pregnant — and, if not pregnant, whether they died willingly or not. She wondered at her own cowardice in running and not trying to take them as well. Not one mention of escape plans had passed her lips. In fact, she never spoke during those few days unless really provoked to do so. Those women hadn't seemed real to her. Now she knew better. Now she'd returned to a city she needed help to escape in the first place. She could pretend it was a rescue mission, but Snickers wouldn't even be here if it wasn't for her and her habit of running away.

Caviar and champagne were set out on a side table. Something niggled at her brain about the brands as she wondered if she should eat.

"I wouldn't," Buddy cautioned as he followed her gaze; then he turned to Stupid. "Actually, don't think we should be here when he arrives; might spoil it for him."

Stupid didn't uncross his arms. "We can't leave her."

Buddy spat, "I ain't playing your game no more. It'll get me killed."

"Then the only choice you really got is by who and how that death happens." Stupid didn't move from the wall.

Buddy, furious now, paced.

"The girl —" Rhiannon tried to interrupt.

Buddy turned on her, bellowing, "Fuck the girl!" And as he took a step her way, Stupid went for his gun.

Then the elevator started moving.

Buddy whirled toward the noise. He looked shocked and terrified, which was odd because he was expecting company. Then he saw Stupid with his gun in hand.

"Holster, you idiot," Buddy mumbled as he watched the elevator. "You'll get all three of us dead."

Stupid holstered his gun and waited. Behind him, a door that was practically hidden in the wall slowly opened.

The driver, followed by two other goon guys, stepped through and slowly crossed up the short hall to the side of Stupid and the elevator. The driver pressed his finger over his lips, and Rhiannon frowned, not even caring what the hell was going on beyond moving forward with this drama.

Stupid saw her reaction and turned in time to get a gun pressed to his head. He sighed, not scared, but like a man unhappy with the task before him.

"What the hell took so long?" Buddy bellowed. "I've been dropping hints all day!"

The two goons relieved Stupid of his gun and grabbed his arms.

The driver cocked his gun, it was one of those ones you had to do that, and Rhiannon thought him a little dense for not doing so ahead of time.

"Not here, fuckwad. The last thing we need to do is mess this up even more." Buddy gestured for them to go back the way they came.

Stupid grinned at her all friendly, and then his eyes turned on Buddy and the grin became evil, snakelike. "I'll be seeing you, Buddy."

"That's right, you will. Take him to the garage and leave the fucker alive until I'm there. Is that the Boss in the elevator?" Buddy asked.

"Nope, sent it up as a distraction. Good thinking, huh?" The driver was pleased.

Buddy wasn't. "Sure, until the Boss wonders why it isn't waiting."

The driver's smile froze, and he, with Stupid and the goons following, practically ran from the room.

Stupid didn't fight them in the least.

The door closed.

Buddy once again turned his back to the elevators. And she knew just by his look that he'd decided the risk of hurting her was worth it.

"Somehow, I don't think Clarence will be the last to die for you," Buddy sneered.

"Care to add yourself to the list?" she quietly warned.

"You tried to help Clarence. You tried to get away. I didn't even touch you." Buddy's eyes glazed a bit with his determined storytelling. "You went through that ..." — he indicated the glass coffee table — "... all by yourself while you were attempting to flee."

She didn't move.

He did.

The elevator doors slid open behind Buddy. She glanced over to see a tall, tuxedo-wearing man carrying a dozen red roses standing inside.

Buddy's grin grew at her glance. "There's no way you are getting past me, bitch." He didn't seem to have noticed that the elevator was occupied. "You're gonna pay for everything your kind ever done to anyone." White-flecked spit had pooled at the edges of his mouth.

Rhiannon couldn't help but notice that as he stalked her, he had an erection. Plus, his command of the English language was seriously deteriorating.

The elevator man frowned and stepped out. He unbuttoned the second button of his tuxedo and freed his gun from his holster.

"We don't have time," Buddy continued to stalk her.

She stopped back-stepping away from him and held her ground. He stepped around the coffee table.

"I feel you worming my head." Buddy was oddly broken. "You got to go before you ruin him —"

Buddy, smashed across the back of the head by Tuxedo's gun, went down like glass shattered on tile. His limbs splayed every which way as he settled into a heap at her feet.

Tuxedo slipped the gun back into its holster and redid

the button. He took only a moment to ascertain that Buddy wasn't getting back up anytime soon, if ever, and then stepped over him.

As Tuxedo's deadened blue eyes rose to lock with hers, Rhiannon's shocked brain suddenly clicked him into past context. She realized she knew him.

Fuck, she'd even fucked him once or twice before she'd realized that fucking your psychotic agent wasn't actually a solid career move. She didn't blame herself; she'd been young at the time, too young for him, actually. Fuck, she'd thought he must have been dead of coke inhalation by now.

He held the roses out with a smile she didn't remember being that white.

"Well, even if it couldn't have been Paris, at least I remembered your favorite flowers." He was as charming as any well-paid leading man. It was a bad line cribbed from a mediocre romantic comedy that had broken box-office records and skyrocketed her Hollywood's way.

Oh, fuck me, Rhiannon thought as everything else, the furniture, the caviar, his tuxedo, clicked into place.

It was all from the movie.

He was the Boss.

He had a script he wanted her to play.

She wasn't going to sweet-talk herself out of this — with Snickers — from someone who'd spent a year in jail for attempted rape. Rape of her.

What were the fucking goddamn chances of it being him, of him being immune, of him being some despot ruler, and her crossing his path?

And fuck her, she just couldn't fucking remember her next line.

IT STARTED TO RAIN. POUR, ACTUALLY. THE rhythmic wipers threatened to put Will to sleep; he was half dreaming of Rhiannon and the shower.

He had spent the day doing Snickers's bidding in the garden, hauling dirt and turning compost. He managed to drive every nail straight. He liked feeling that tired. It was the exhaustion of being well used, of being productive, like it was actually possible to do something useful.

He hadn't heard her come in, but he had heard the toilet lid open and had said, a little sharp, "Don't flush, Snickers!"

Rhiannon laughed. That deep throaty laugh, the laugh he'd actually begun trying to figure out ways to get from her.

He was very aware that only a thin plastic curtain separated them. He wondered whether if he asked her, she would join him; if she would let him suck the water from where it might pool between her neck and collarbone.

The cool breeze called his attention to the fact that

Rhiannon, still sitting on the toilet, had pulled the shower curtain back with her foot.

He wiped the water that poured across his face as he straightened his head from underneath the nozzle.

He looked at her looking at him.

There wasn't anything else he could do in that moment; wasn't anything else he wanted to do.

He never thought to move or cover or speak.

Though the action was playful, her face was so serious, so guarded, as she ran her eyes up the profile of his legs, ass, and chest to his face. But once they had eye contact, she slowly smiled: a wicked, full-of-promise smile. She laughed again, then laughed more when he shivered from it.

"Don't drop the soap," she teased.

He raised his eyebrow the way he was pretty sure she liked. Her grin widened from wicked to something else.

She didn't take her eyes off him as she lowered her leg and let the curtain fall back into place, then eventually stood.

He waited, literally holding his breath, to see if she would make good on the smile. He could see her shadow through the curtain.

She seemed to be waiting.

Was his offer not clear enough?

He glanced down.

Nope, he was pretty sure it was pretty clear he wanted her.

B.B. barked nearby, maybe on the stairs; and where there was B.B. there was sure to be Snickers.

Rhiannon turned to quickly exit the bathroom, but not before she flushed the goddamn toilet.

The next day, Will had the brilliant idea of taking a little scouting trip with the girls, and they all knew how well that had worked out.

SHE WASN'T TOTALLY SURE HE COULD IDENTIFY her. Maybe he actually thought she was the character in the movie rather than Rhiannon Wells. He'd had her made up like her last magazine cover, but the film he was referencing was from ten years ago.

She took the flowers and smelled them; she remembered that, at least. Milking the dramatic pause while she racked her brain for her next line. It was a scene from the very end of the movie, the reunification of the lovers. A sex scene was next, the thought of which made her stomach churn. She imagined that was when the bedroom came into play, and she wasn't sure how to avoid that... she was still hoping Snickers was nearby. Her character... her character wasn't this easily swayed. His character had to pass a test... his character had done something wrong.

She looked up to see if he would give her a hint.

The dark look that passed across his perfectly constructed — as in plastic — chiseled features didn't bode well for her not remembering her cues.

Fuck.

She couldn't get the thought of Snickers out of her head, and this was blocking every other memory she tried to access.

Plus, she never saw the fucking movies more than once after she made them.

"Roses, caviar, and champagne," she blurted suddenly. "Is that the best you can do?" Rhiannon arched an eyebrow and turned slightly away from him.

He smiled and rattled off the next line. "That's just the dressing. I'm the main course."

He reached for her hand and she avoided him.

The entire scene came flooding back. The brain was a powerful thing when put to the test. She hadn't heard these lines in over ten years.

"Cocky, aren't you? So secure that you can have me back just like that, with a snap of your fingers... that I'm even still interested."

"You're here, aren't you? You must be interested, even if you are just here to break my heart, again."

She snorted and said with utter conviction, "Like you even have a heart to break."

She turned away from him to look out the window.

He wrapped his hands around her bare shoulders, and she tried not to shudder with revulsion.

Night had fallen completely, wiping out all identifying landscape. This could be any city, any time.

"I know this isn't the view you remember, that you expected, but it's what we have, and I'd like to have it together, just with you," he whispered into her neck, and she could feel the slight rain of spit when he spoke, over-enunciating.

She couldn't figure a way out.

And what the hell did that last line mean anyway?

Fucking writers with their fucking love of twisty wordings that, in the end, meant fucking nothing.

She wrapped her arms around herself before she remembered she was supposed to press her hands against the window before her next line.

He froze behind her and gripped her arms a little too tightly.

She slowly dropped her hands and stepped closer to the window.

He let her go, willing to ignore her lapse.

She pressed her palms to the glass. "How are we to continue with this between us?" she asked.

He spun her around and away from the window.

"Don't you see?" he cried, impassioned. "There is nothing between us but our own stupidity."

"Are you calling me stupid?" She willed enraged tears to the surface of her eyes and, while struggling to do so, wished she were hydrated.

"No, no! It's me. I'm the stupid one. I never should have left. I can't live without you, no matter who or what you've done in the past."

"Who I've done? What are you accusing me of?" she wailed dramatically.

"Him! Him! I know all about the wealthy Frenchman!" He paced.

"Frenchman? What are you talking about?" she asked, suddenly aware that they were very close to the end of the scene and nearer the bedding part.

"All that matters is I forgive you. I want you, no matter what!" He gripped her upper arms again, which was definitely something she didn't remember from the movie.

"How dare you. You think... you think I slept with

someone else?" She took a step back, out of his arms, to ready the next part of the scene.

"You didn't?" He played confused well.

She hauled off — this was her favorite part of romantic comedies — and slapped him across the face. She hit him harder than she ever would have hit another actor, putting everything she could — what with the broken ribs and high heels — into it.

He stood still, maybe in shock, with his face turned from her. Then his hand rose — so typically— to touch his scorched cheek.

Then he looked at her.

His lips stretched across his teeth, but he wasn't smiling. His eyes burned like he didn't recognize her or that part of the scene.

She waited, her slap hand pressed to her heaving bosom, not that she was out of breath, but because that was what the director had wanted. She watched the fog of rage slowly ease from his eyes and face.

He stared at her breasts.

She wondered if she should prompt his next line.

"How could you think that of me?" she whispered, skipping his line.

His eyes shot from her chest to her face, but he accepted the prompt.

"I was just so jealous, and Sue said..." He wasn't completely back into the scene, and she wondered if the slap was a big or small mistake.

"Sue!" she bleated. "Your precious Sue said!" Rhiannon flung herself away and he, just like in the movie, grabbed her waist and pulled her back.

"You are jealous!" He was, happily, back into the role.

"Never," she vowed. She tried to twist away, but soon was tangled in his arms.

What was it with romantic comedies and all this lying and grabbing? Love wasn't like that in real life; in real life it was —

He was staring at her.

Had she missed a line?

No, but his smile was gone.

Then she remembered she was supposed to initiate the kiss. Rhiannon had kissed lots of people she didn't love. In fact, she was now sure she'd never truly loved anyone before the virus, but this was different. There were no cameras. She wasn't acting with free will. Also, she was sure this wasn't going to be a fake-as-much-as-possible sex scene. Still... a taunt of *Snickers, Snickers, Snickers* ran through her head.

She fisted bunches of his tuxedo lapels and tilted her head as if giving in.

He slammed his mouth onto hers, just as hard as she had slapped him. He yanked her head back by her hair, a move also not in the movie. She tried to stay relaxed as she pressed her body along his. He wasn't aroused, *thank God... but, on second thought, maybe that was a bad thing.* She had to take control somehow, but how was that possible when she was supposed to be playing a vapid, passive, two-dimensional character?

"Shall... shall we... seal this deal in the bedroom?" she murmured against his teeth and jabbing tongue, hoping to recall him to the scene.

"I want you, you know I do, but are you sure? Are you sure this is a deal you want to make with me, forever?" He stumbled around the words. "That's the way I want you, forever. I won't take you any other way." He recited the lines, but just wasn't into the scene as written anymore.

He gripped her too tightly and was wrecking her dress, makeup, and hair, all huge no-no's on a set. She could actually feel his control slipping. He either couldn't maintain the facade now that he was actually in the scene, or what was taking place didn't fit with what was in his head. Either way, Rhiannon sensed she didn't have much time. So she turned her head to the double doors that led to the bedroom.

He followed her gaze.

He smiled in that deadened way she wished people would stop doing. Maybe they'd always done so, but it seemed to be an epidemic nowadays.

He released her. She figured that, if she bothered to look, there would be new bruises forming on her arms soon.

Is he testing my follow-through? She wasn't about to deviate from the script now, especially without a weapon. This reminded her of Buddy, who she realized she'd completely forgotten about, and she glanced in his direction.

Except Buddy wasn't on the floor anymore. He was on his feet, gun in hand, but swaying in the same way she imagined his injured brain was swimming. The gun arched from her to the Boss, who seemed unconcerned at this development, and back again. Buddy was blocking her bedroom cross.

"Were you thinking of going somewhere?" the Boss murmured to her in his best sexy voice.

An improvised line, which was fine, except —

Except Buddy seemed to be attempting to bring the gun around to solidly point at her, and that was more than a bit distracting.

Still, she was a professional, so she took a couple of steps that angled away from Buddy but toward what she guessed were the bedroom doors.

Unfortunately, her movement made it easier for Buddy to home in, so that, as she turned to throw a come-hither look over her shoulder, he fired.

She froze and waited for the bullet to puncture her while dimly aware that if it was going to, she should have felt it already.

Buddy took aim again.

The Boss sighed, pulled his gun from his holster, leveled it, and shot Buddy in the gut. He never once looked anywhere but at her.

Buddy looked blankly surprised at this development. He pondered the blood spreading across his stomach. Then he dropped his gun.

The Boss tucked his gun away and continued to watch her as if waiting for her to pick up the scene, as if a man wasn't dying right beside him.

The close-range blast had done damage, and she tried to look away from what might be bits of Buddy's intestines slipping through his fingers.

Buddy gave up on putting himself together and stumbled toward the Boss, falling against his side with a rapturous gaze and mewing, "Why, why?"

Even as Buddy pawed to grasp his tuxedo, the Boss's gaze didn't break from what Rhiannon was sure was her horrified face.

Actually, he, the Boss, was almost vibrating, jangling with the thrill of watching her watch Buddy slide to the floor and bleed out.

She couldn't watch anymore, didn't want to accept that the Boss was more turned on by her watching him kill than he was by kissing her.

If he could kill a devoted follower —

She whip-turned, but stumbled when her stride didn't part the fabric that wrapped around her legs.

She managed not to fall.

She flung herself through into the bedroom.

She flung herself away from the responsibility of Buddy's death.

She flung herself away from all the death to come, all the death she saw in the beads of sweat on the Boss's forehead, the kind you get from a great orgasm.

The bedroom was really just the next level of hell. And not just for her, because Snickers was there.

Snickers, her face white and blank and her hair ribbons pretty and pink, sat in the middle of the bed with a monster chained to either side.

IT WAS THE MIDDLE OF THE NIGHT, BUT THEY needed more gas, fuel actually, because he was pretty sure the tank took diesel. They had scheduled scouts, diviners, to go ahead of the group and check out gas stations. It was a risky job; you never knew what you'd run into, and though Will had signed up, his name had never been drawn for this duty. On his third try, Dale had found full tanks conveniently located on the highway. Problem was they just had to figure out how to turn them back on.

Nearby, a sign declared them on the outskirts of a town named Hope, but it was the sign that read 'Vancouver 150 km' that interested him more. Course, he couldn't translate kilometers to miles and neither could Big. Even Boomer was American originally, not that that wasn't obvious. Turned out eventually that Rav was the only one from their group who was originally from this area, and 150 kilometers was approximately ninety miles. Will briefly thought it odd that the Canadian knew the conversion when the Americans didn't, but was more focused in how long ninety miles took.

"About an hour and a half?" he asked Big, who shrugged and took a long look at the four-lane highway that stretched between here and there.

"Highway's completely blocked. If people had just stayed home to die, we'd be able to move easy. Now, don't know, six hours?"

"Moving always feels better than standing still," he said, but Big just snorted at anything that didn't ease the inconvenience they faced.

"At least it's a full moon. We can see a bit. Moving all those cars... well, you know. Ah, the boys got the pumps working; hope there's enough gas to keep us going." Big moved off.

Some gas stations had kill switches for their pumps, which most conscientious employees seemed to have tripped before dying. Issue was that some of them were coded or alarmed, so you never knew if you could get the pumps running again. The portable generators they'd dragged through the mountains helped. Will hadn't thought of that himself, even with all his collecting and stocking; gas was easier to come by outside the city centers. Course, he'd also never needed to fuel an attack force, tank and all.

He never had much to do with this handy herd of men around him. He'd grown accustomed to bending his back to get things done, and he missed it. Oh, if he pushed it, they let him operate the tow truck — it was his, after all — and they certainly expected that he had a plan of some sort.

If this highway was plugged with vehicles between here and Vancouver, he thought Big was being optimistic about it taking only six hours. He wished he could feel more confident that Rhiannon and Snickers had six more hours. He glanced over at One Ear huddled in the back of the pickup with B.B.

One Ear hadn't spoken much, if any, against his Boss; and in that silence, Will recognized fear. The closer the city got, the more silent One Ear went. Ultimately, he was more afraid of the Boss than his present circumstances, which was a red flag to heed in more than one way. First, that fear seen in an ally and mixed with such loyalty meant there was a good chance this Boss was insane as well as evil. So what would Rhiannon, who was rash when afraid, do when confronted with crazy and evil?

She wouldn't run or hide without Snickers. Will wasn't being judgmental, just pragmatic about how quickly it could go from bad to worse. Could be it had gone worse already. The second red flag was One Ear himself. *What levels of betrayal was he capable of? Hell, it wouldn't even be betrayal, seeing as we're enemies.* So he had to assume they were driving right into a trap that Buddy and Boss would collude to spring, and that Stupid had probably already paid with his life. None of those possibilities made him want to get to the city any slower.

He left the gassing of the tow truck to Rav and wandered over to Boomer and the tank. Big crossed the lot to follow him. Boomer had scored a baseball hat for some hockey team — maybe the Canucks if they'd recently gotten a new logo — from the gas station's convenience store.

"There's a wide median on either side of the highway," he pointed out to Boomer.

Boomer nodded, spit, but once his throat was clear, said, "Not wide enough for Delilah."

"And, Tex, there's no way people didn't pull over in

some spots, maybe to stop and die, maybe to try to get around the gridlock," Big added.

"But it is wide like that all the way through the valley, until you get to the bridges, that is," Rav piped up from behind as he joined them.

Will was quiet and they all let him think, like they always did. The diesel glugged into the tank, and he wondered how many gallons it took.

"But if you positioned Delilah just right between the cars, and if we cleared a stretch so you could get up speed, then ..." — he tried to not think of all the families in all those cars — "... then you could use her like a battering ram, with the medians to push into."

"Sure could, Tex," Boomer eagerly responded.

"Might have to stop and clear spots in places, but we could move faster that way," Big added.

Will moved a couple of steps away to think about it further; only Big followed.

"You're not worried about being disrespectful of the dead anymore, Tex?" Big asked.

He tried to look through the darkness to see how many cars, how many dead bodies, they were about to disturb; but in the end, his own fear won.

"The lives that hang in the balance are more important now than the husks of the dearly departed." He finally gave voice to his decision.

"I agree. Plus, once we've won the city, you can just tell people to come back to clean up." Big liked to plan their victory and rule ahead.

It made him ill — a feeling he was unfortunately getting accustomed to — thinking of tossing dead bodies, dead families, around like garbage. He, in pure denial, had spent a lot of time carefully erasing the effects of the virus on his life and the environment of the town and surrounding area.

When Snickers — even with her muteness and other not-so-obvious signs of trauma — and then Rhiannon arrived, he thought they could just exist. Exist in the cocoon he'd built, but life wasn't like that. Life made you get your hands dirty; life was vengeful if you tried an easy route.

"This is just the way it is," he told Big, who didn't answer. Then he turned to nod to Boomer, who rewarded this decision with a toothy grin.

He clapped Big on the shoulder, a gesture the man often employed himself. Big seemed to like his use of it.

"Everyone restocked?" he asked.

"You had us covered in town, Tex, but yeah, I think everyone has stretched and shit by now," Big answered.

The others — God, how many was he leading to death he didn't even know — had gathered around the tank in conference with Boomer and Rav.

He turned to the tow truck, knowing that Big would convey his so-called orders. They all got it anyway, like a collective consciousness.

Rav stepped up to match his stride, but continued on when Will paused to pet B.B. She wagged her nonexistent tail. One Ear looked to be sleeping.

Behind him, Boomer fired up the tank.

He was so close he could taste it, taste blood and ashes with a swirl of strawberry. But he was hoping that was just his imagination.

SHE FALTERED.

Rhiannon could admit it, even if just to herself. She saw Snickers with her white, blank face and she just stopped to stare.

Perhaps it was the flanking monsters, two of the Infected, one of which unfolded from its wall slump to practically seven feet tall when she entered the room.

Perhaps it was the doll clothing — *please, please don't let it have been he who undressed and redressed her* — or Snickers's falsely rouged cheeks.

But, no, the truth: it was because she thought she was too late. She saw no life in Snickers. The girl didn't even respond to her name.

"Snickers? Snickers, babe, you okay?" she whispered. And for the first time, she wished she knew the child's real name and then thought she was an awful person to not have tried to learn it before.

Snickers, cross-legged in the bed in her frilly pink dress, continued to stare blankly, even though Rhiannon was sure she was in her sight line.

She finally managed to trigger her feet and take a stumbling step forward, only to have the Infected rattle their chains in anticipation.

Snickers was completely trapped; maybe only their fingertips could brush her, but no one was getting near the bed with them guarding it.

Voices from the other room reminded her that this reunion scene was about to be interrupted by something she didn't want Snickers to witness. That had to be his plan: have Snickers watch and then make Rhiannon watch as he killed the child once he realized that rape alone just didn't do it for him.

She looked for a weapon. The Infected watched her; Snickers didn't.

Just get her out of here and everything will be back to normal, she told herself. Of course, this all might have just compounded whatever trauma had caused the child's muteness. *What if Snickers's brain had shut down for good?*

The lamp was bolted to the dresser recently.

The drawers were empty.

Pulling back the curtains revealed that the windows were barred.

Fuck.

This was a prison — recently renovated — to house her. Silk/cotton sheets on the bed. A favorite soap by the soaker tub. See's Candies on the table. And not a single, obvious thing she could use for a weapon.

Thank God she was resourceful in a pinch, because it was about to get tight in here.

She could hear the Boss issuing some series of orders in the next room, which she gathered had to do with Buddy's body and dinner.

Asparagus did indeed seem to be an issue worth killing over.

Rhiannon returned to the middle of the room so Snickers, if she could register images anymore, could see her. Then she did something she never did. She waited. She wasn't going to be able to figure herself out of this ahead of time; she was going to have to act in the moment.

The Boss strolled in. He'd removed his bloodstained jacket and loosened his tie, perhaps hoping to look dashing; but rather, he looked... *weak*.

She smiled at this thought. This seemed to off-balance him, and she wondered at her own stupidity in forgetting the weapon she always had.

The doors, propelled by unseen hands, closed. She tried not to think about the fact that more guards equaled more obstacles to their escape; plus, now she'd have a catatonic child in tow.

She widened the smile and his step actually faltered.

"Hello," she murmured, knowing it wouldn't take more than one word to seal the spell.

The idea was to get him in her grasp; then she'd go all black widow.

Except they, the Infected, chose that moment to rattle their chains and — as they stretched their arms to the Boss — sniff the air. He stopped and stared.

Fuck! Fuck! Fuck! Buddy's blood must have stained more than the tuxedo jacket.

The Boss shook his head and then looked at Snickers.

"How pretty our daughter looks," he said as he turned to her.

Ah, fuck, he had another script for her now, one she really didn't know.

"This is absolutely insane!" She turned to scratch his eyes out, to get the confrontation over with, but he was faster and stronger than her.

Before she knew it, he had her twisted on the bed with the gun at the base of her skull and her face inches from Snickers, who didn't react.

His knee at the small of her back pressed her pelvis to the bed while he dragged her, sharply arched backwards, by the hair. And then Them. They reached, brushing with pudgy, swollen fingertips against her face, across Snickers's face and shoulder. They moaned and slurped.

He just held her there, not speaking. Her ribs screamed with pain if she struggled, and any movement seemed to arouse the Infected more.

She saw nothing in Snickers, no flicker of recognition; the girl had retreated into the depths of her mind, and those brushing fingers were what had driven her.

The taunting words *your fault, your fault* started up in Rhiannon's head again.

She stopped struggling.

He didn't loosen his grip.

She thought about loss and how it had never really meant anything until now, because now there was no anger. Just soul-aching sadness.

She gave up.

She gave in.

He let go of her.

She sank her head into Snickers's lap and cried.

She cried for this child who'd almost been hers.

She cried for the sound of B.B.'s happy bark the day she chased that raccoon out of the sun-dappled, newly seeded garden.

She cried for Will, absolutely everything that was

perfect and right about Will, and how losing Snickers was going to kill him.

She cried knowing that, just by being her, she'd ruined it all. Except this went beyond self-pity into a craterous cavern of dark despair.

She felt something different brush her cheek. *Tiny fingers this time?* It didn't repeat, but it dried her tears in record time.

Rhiannon looked up at Snickers, but the child didn't move again, if she had moved at all; only the pudgy fingertips and moaning persisted.

She straightened out of their reach, and never taking her eyes off Snickers, smoothed her hair and readjusted her dress.

"I thought the pink would bring out the touch of amber of her eyes." This was a blatant lie, pink did no such thing, but what did he know, really? In the end, crazy or not, he was just a man, and she had never let any man get the best of her, no matter how hard or soft or long they tried. This was his second attempt, and she was going to make him pay for it.

He'd been waiting for her, not an emotion on his face.

"Ah, Rhiannon. Self-preservation was always your best look," he said.

She pulled her eyes from Snickers.

She turned to him.

He was seated next to the window, its curtains drawn again, eating chocolates.

Her chocolates.

She adopted that slight slouch: the one that got her that ten-million-dollar perfume contract and was soon after copied by supermodels worldwide.

She sauntered into the bathroom, leaving the door open so he could see she was just fixing her makeup. Her mascara hadn't run. Perfect.

He accepted this and moved on. "I've been rather unhappy without you two here with me. But now that you are here, all will be well."

"Of course you have," she replied, and her voice took on the resonance of the tiled bathroom. "We two were utterly lost without you."

The Boss laughed; but when Rhiannon exited the bathroom, she didn't like that he now seemed to be fixated on Snickers.

She leaned against the dresser. As she reached down to remove one of her shoes, the strap of her dress fell enough to expose the top of her breast. That got his attention. It was a difficult game to seduce a man who would prefer to take by force what you had to offer. Utter submission was your last card.

She massaged her foot, allowing her dress to hike up and reveal plenty of thigh.

"I'm surprised by your affection for the child," he said.

She switched feet, removed the other shoe, rubbed and replied as if still in the middle of thinking about it. "Hmm, a passing fancy, maybe? I... everything had gone crazy and there was this child who needed me, and maybe I would never get a chance..." She let the thought dangle.

She, her shoes hooked in her fingers, took a step toward him as if hesitant, but he stood as if fully expecting her to complete the cross.

She didn't move.

He grinned, into the game.

She delicately chewed her lower lip, drawing his eyes there, and then turned her head as if shy.

He came to her, closing the gap quicker than she anticipated, so her momentary shock was real and delighted him.

"A baby, hey?" he asked. "All Rhiannon Wells wants in this big, free-for-the-taking world is a baby? Well, you've come to the right place." He laughed. "My baby."

She swayed as if she couldn't stand without him, and he bought it.

"I'm so happy you are still you," she whispered in his ear.

He shivered.

And this time, there was no mistaking the stiff dick.

She brushed her fingers across his lips and then kissed him lightly, lightly, lightly...

He moaned, he closed his eyes, and then she bit his fucking lip.

He shrieked; blood spurted.

He tried to tear away, but that made it worse.

He boxed her ears and the pain of it caused her to bite through his lip; a hunk of it came off in her mouth.

He howled and twisted away.

She couldn't walk properly from the ringing in her ears, and she ended up on all fours, spitting out lip and blood at the base of the bed.

She was vaguely aware of the amped moans from the monster duo and that the Boss had calmed enough to inspect his face in the dresser mirror.

The room churned; she couldn't find her feet.

He came at her then, and if that particular rib hadn't been broken before, it was after his kick.

She hit the foot of the bed and then fell back to all fours.

He liked this position and leaned over her doggie style to fumble with the dress. He tried to part her thighs, but she was strong there.

The room settled a bit.

He decided he had enough access anyway and went for his belt.

She smashed her skull into his nose.

More blood.

But he didn't stumble much.

He got her around the back of the neck and slammed her head into the floor. She was thankful the carpet was plush, and relaxed into it for a moment. This concerned him, and he leaned over to make sure she wasn't out of the game.

Suddenly he cursed and started to scramble over the bed.

He's after Snickers, her brain informed her body, and then she was on her feet. It took her a second to piece together the scene and realize that Snickers had managed to get her hands on the Boss's gun when he leaned over.

The Infected, enraged by the blood, were making it almost impossible for the Boss to get his hands on Snickers, who was grappling with the big gun.

Snickers got the weapon turned around in her hands and pointed at the Boss.

He froze.

Snickers squeezed the trigger and nothing happened.

"Try a little harder." The Boss laughed.

Snickers steadied her aim and squeezed again just as one of the Infected knocked the gun from her hands.

The Boss, still laughing, caught Snickers's foot and dragged her, kicking and fighting, off the bed.

The Infected wanted in on the grabbing as well.

The Boss, completely focused on Snickers, turned to violently vault the girl across the room. Instead, he discovered the three-inch-heel of Rhiannon's previously so impractical shoe buried in his throat, which was a bitch, as she'd aimed for his eye.

He stumbled, but she managed to snag Snickers before he dropped her. He was momentarily down but not completely out of the fight.

Of course, the next problem was the Infected. They were tired of all this blood going around with none for them. So they snapped their chains. Well, so far, only one chain each, but they were each at work on the second.

Rhiannon scrambled for the door, but realized Snickers wasn't with her.

The child was crawling underneath one of the Infected to try to get at the gun.

The Boss had yanked the shoe heel from his throat.

"FUCK! FUCK! FUCK!"

Snickers looked back and Rhiannon realized — it was a moment for realizations — that she had yelled that out loud.

There was a knock at the door.

"Boss?" a male voice asked. "Everything okay?"

The Boss struggled upright with the help of a bedpost and, at the same time, struggled to speak.

Snickers laid hands on the gun just as the Infected snapped the second chain.

The first one went after the Boss; covered in blood, he was an obvious choice.

The second swiped at Snickers, who rolled under the bed.

Thus foiled, it came at Rhiannon.

It was fucking fast.

It backed her into the bathroom.

In fact, it smashed her right through the glass shower, only to drop her amid all that glass and then seem oddly confused about its leg.

Snickers, with gun, stood at the entrance of the bathroom. She shot the monster again, in the chest this time, which got its attention. It growled.

Rhiannon crawled, ignoring the glass, to the toilet. She grabbed the tank cover and, glad it was a pompously large bathroom with room to swing —

She smashed it across the monster's head.

It went down.

Gunfire erupted in the bedroom.

Snickers hid underneath the sink.

Rhiannon retrieved the lid; she'd lost it in her first strike.

She bludgeoned the Infected a few more times. Between the tile and the tank lid, its brains were mush.

Then she crept to the door to look out. Snickers snagged her hand but stayed under the sink.

Three men huddled around the prone form of the Boss. The other Infected was lying nearby.

The Boss's legs moved, and Rhiannon must have moaned because Snickers's grip got more intense. She wondered how many bullets were left in the gun.

She reached down for Snickers, and the girl climbed into her arms like a monkey. She turned her around so she could cling to her back, and then took the gun.

Then she slipped out of the bathroom and made a beeline for the bedroom doors.

Someone yelled, "Hey!" behind her, but she kept on going.

As she hit the living room, a series of thoughts went through her head:

A. Buddy was gone.

B. They'd even cleaned up his blood.

C. The elevators were too slow; and

D. She could really use a swig of that champagne.

She sprinted toward the far door, through which the driver had dragged Stupid earlier.

Shouts came from behind her.

Her escape route door slammed open, and with two guns blazing, Stupid stepped through.

She ducked, praying he wouldn't hit Snickers, but he wasn't aiming for her. No answering shots came; they hadn't expected friendly fire.

Rhiannon didn't know what the fuck was going on, but as always, true to herself, she didn't give a fuck. So when she stood, she brought her gun into play.

Her first shot didn't hit; Snickers off-balanced her.

Stupid cringed and held his guns up as if surrendering.

"Strawberry plant," he yelled.

Which was odd enough to give her pause. He risked a look at her and saw her waiting.

"Tex, sent me... well, sort of... he... you... left your strawberry plant," he stuttered to explain, but kept his hands in surrender position. "I'm Clarence. Will calls me Stupid, but he doesn't mean it anymore."

So Stupid was a mole. Will had sent him... but wait, why not come himself?

Her doubt must have shown, because Stupid added, "He's on his way."

She stepped forward and gifted Stupid with a blazing smile that nearly knocked him off his feet. His face went all slack.

"Rhiannon Wells, I've wanted you since I was sixteen years old," he breathed.

"Get over it," she replied, and hitched Snickers higher on her back.

He did.

He'd thought about abandoning the tank a bunch of times even before they hit the bridge; bridges, he corrected himself with a groan. Storming a city without a tank would have little effect, except there'd be less bad-guy bloodshed, whereas they, the supposed good guys, would all be slaughtered.

He kept trying to actually listen to what Big told him, about the breeding factories and dead women, but Will really was in this for his girls.

His girls.

Anyway, the bridges slowed them. There was no simple way to shove cars off into the river through steel beams and girders. So they reverted, using the tow truck or moving cars under their own steam if possible. The Port Mann Bridge spanned 2,093 meters, 6,866 feet. It bothered him that Rav knew that and also thought, erroneously, that Will would like the knowledge. A lot of cars fit into four lanes over 6,800 feet. He'd glared at Rav until he went away, but not before Rav had started to estimate how many cars blocked them from the other side of the river.

He pulled the dead husk — not registering sex or age or anything — from behind the wheel of the next car and reminded himself they only needed two lanes clear to get the trucks across. The tank, of course, could have simply driven over just about anything in its path, but they couldn't move an army with just one tank.

Sunrise was well dawned, which was helpful for the fact that they could now really see what they were doing, but made Will even more tense about the time stretching between him and his girls.

As he looked up from the car he was trying to start, he noticed all the others fanned out in front of him. Many more people were with them now. Their numbers had continually swelled.

Why hadn't these people fled once they'd gotten out of the city, and why were they willing to head back into occupied territory now?

He'd expected to be attacked as they got closer, maybe by small outposts, as that was how he would have set up exterior defenses if it had been his city to secure.

It was mostly men joining, so maybe Big wasn't exaggerating about the genocide of women.

They were now, given the devastated population, a large force.

These volunteers didn't seem scared or intimidated. They often just stepped out in twos or threes from the fields or buildings and sought out Big.

Later, they would often try to catch Will's eye or clap his shoulder as they moved to their assigned tasks. They didn't engage him further.

He was accustomed, way back, to being a touchstone. The quarterback often was, but this was different. *It's not a game anymore.*

He spent much time with maps and Rav. Few routes led into the city, especially for a tank. Downtown was the goal, according to One Ear.

Boomer complained more than once about the lack of gun stores en route, but so far — despite the Canadian peacekeeper reputation — they had more than enough guns and ammo to go around.

Will tried to figure a way to minimize their impact on the city, but this was a road map of an extinct society; it told him nothing of the now.

He also put very little faith in One Ear's hand-drawn map, and even though he worried about wasting precious time, he wasn't stupid enough to follow its suggested route into downtown.

From here, he could see skyscrapers in the downtown core, and he wondered if Rhiannon knew he was close. He hoped to God she did and would wait. Course, he knew he didn't have a hope in hell that she'd hide out waiting for him to blaze in and save the day, but he still silently prayed.

Plus, Snickers was usually reasonable if she wasn't armed. Actually, the thought of her being reasonable or unarmed didn't really comfort. He hoped she was armed and completely unreasonable; and sick though it might be, that made him smile, which made everyone around him smile.

They were going to kick some ass and save their women. This was what men were made to do, whether you believed in God or Darwin. He just hoped, once more, that he wasn't too late and that he didn't make things worse by storming the castle.

A feral growl snapped him out of his head pretty quick, but not quick enough to avoid the body that lunged across the back seat or the knife suddenly at his neck. He had left the driver's side door open, and they, he and his attacker, tumbled out of it and hit the pavement. Will tried to twist away while the creature on top of him tried to slice his neck open. It took him precious seconds to realize the following:

A. The creature was actually a man. A scrawny, unnaturally strong man, though that strength might be fueled by the feverish rage that seemed contrary to the tears streaming down his almost skeletonized face.

B. He'd barely managed to block the first strike of the knife and could, in fact, feel it cutting into the flesh of his throat.

C. He was going to die within spitting distance of Rhiannon and Snickers.

Then in the moment that he acknowledged the possibility of his own death, someone booted the salivating, manic creature off him. Though it quickly turned out that this abrupt intervention wasn't exactly a smart move. Will recognized Big's boot and pant leg — Big favored desert army fatigues — just as he felt the knife slit completely through the skin of his neck.

He clutched his throat.

Big stepped across him to boot the creature a second time.

Will struggled to his feet, but with all the others grabbing and pressing him back, he couldn't even manage to get to his knees.

The creature, having lost the knife, launched itself at Big with its teeth as weapons; and seeing this, Will realized what was wrong with the man.

"Don't let him bite you, Big," he tried to say, and was rewarded for this effort by warm blood flushing through his fingers.

"He's rabid. Rabid. Rabid." He didn't realize he'd been repeating himself until Rav's voice cut through the din.

"We got it, Tex. Now you've got to let us help you," Rav pleaded. "Tex, you let go, let go of your neck. I've got it."

"Just a scratch," he croaked, and he could hear Big's booming laugh in response. Rav looked a little pissed at them both.

"It's not just a scratch. You got to let us help," Rav reiterated.

This finally seemed, to his foggy, blood-deprived brain, like solid advice, so he let Rav tend to the neck wound.

Big's face swam in the air above him.

"We'll put him down, Tex. Humane thing," Big informed him.

"He's just protecting his family. I disturbed them," Will tried to say, but Big had moved away. He struggled to make himself heard, but all those hands were pressing him down again, and Rav looked more scared than pissed now.

"Big. Big," Will called until he focused on Big's face again. Big stood over the creature, who cowered and wept, though he seemed unable to actually speak or even swallow. *End stages of the disease, then,* his brain randomly informed him, though he had no idea where he got that knowledge.

"We keep moving," he ordered the big man.

"Always, Tex," Big answered.

And as edges of black exhaustion threatened to take his sight, he watched Big shoot the man point-blank in the brain. He could have sworn he saw a moment of clarity precede the fatal wound and then relief flood the dying man's face and body as he bled out on the pavement.

TOO MUCH TIME HAD PASSED.

Stupid had insisted on securing the penthouse before they could flee so they'd know no one was at their backs. While this was logical, Rhiannon chafed at staying or keeping Snickers in this plush prison any longer than absolutely necessary.

They had debated killing the Boss, who'd managed to get some packing into his neck wound and not bleed out yet. They secured him in the bedroom to get him out of Snickers's sight. But, when retribution won over hostage benefits and Stupid had gone to put him down, they discovered an open door leading into an empty adjoining suite. They didn't take time to investigate.

She worried about all this death traumatizing Snickers further, but the child looked resolute and content as long as Rhiannon remained in physical contact.

Stupid also insisted on bandaging the shower-glass cuts on her hands, knees, and lower legs, as well as various other patching. She'd submitted.

He gathered the guns into a bag made from a tablecloth.

She ate as much of the dinner laid out in the living room as she could keep down.

Snickers preferred the crackers that went with the caviar.

They didn't open the champagne.

When Stupid felt ready, they hit the back stairs. The concrete was cold on her bare feet, but her heels would have slowed her. Plus the dress, which was oddly intact, dragged enough already.

Stupid took point, with Snickers next. Rhiannon hadn't wanted to put the child on her own feet, but thought it was better to conserve energy now.

They made quick work of the stairs; Stupid had obviously navigated them twice already, but they hit a bit of an obstacle in the parking garage. Namely, a small herd of them, the Infected. Stupid swore when he saw them milling about, loose among the cars.

"What is it?" she hissed.

He had her peek around the steel door to make her own assessment.

"What are those, fucking guard dogs?" she growled.

Stupid shrugged.

"Does he usually have them roaming loose like that?" she asked.

"Nope," Stupid responded and then waited, like a good soldier, for orders.

"So a sudden change in protocol isn't a good sign," she mused. When Stupid looked confused, she added, "They know we're on the run. You were right; we should have killed the Boss right away." She hated being wrong.

Stupid shrugged again; that was really going to bother her eventually. He seemed to take her glare in stride. His apologetic smile reminded her that he was just the muscle, and she had to be the brains.

"So... a car is out, and I imagine hitting the street on foot is a bad idea." She thought of the mob that had quickly formed the last time.

Stupid nodded but also eyed Snickers, who was trying to sneak a look into the garage. He delicately unwove her fingers from the door latch.

"How hard is it going to be to get out of the hotel and into another building without being seen?" Rhiannon asked Stupid.

"Not," he answered.

Stupid headed back up the stairs. She, with a sigh, followed, not too sure how many more steps she was going to be able to manage. Then Snickers tucked a hand in hers, and she knew she'd go as far as she was needed.

They cut through the kitchen, crossed twenty feet through a dumpster-filled alley, and entered an adjacent building. They were still in the hotel.

The decor of this brick building, though still high-end, obviously dated back to the '80s. *Whoever thought green and peach went well together?*

They continued to follow exit signs; and after endless turns of hallways, they found themselves in an even older, maybe unused, part of the hotel.

Furniture storage seemed to be the main function of these rooms.

She broke the silence and asked Stupid, "Do you still know where we are?"

He shook his head no, but answered, "Heading east."

Dust had settled on the baseboards. The carpet was worn down the middle of the hall.

Just as Rhiannon started wondering how they hadn't seen anyone else, three unidentified Red Jackets burst in and then shoved by them to flee down the corridor. They stopped to gape after the trio, who actually fell over each other to slam into and out of a steel exit door at the far end of the hall.

"That's not good." Stupid voiced what they must all be thinking.

She crossed to pick up Snickers; the Red Jackets had shoved her off her feet. As she reached for the child, the hotel rumbled and then shook enough to knock her down, but it was the second and third rumble that did damage.

The shaking continued, and as plaster started cracking and falling, Rhiannon pulled Snickers into a doorway and curled her body around the child.

She looked up to see Stupid farther along the hall, but trying to get back to them.

Cracked wall plaster revealed brick beyond, and then those bricks started falling.

Stupid took refuge in his own doorway just as the third boom — or perhaps bomb — shook the building so hard that the floor cracked open. Dropped, actually.

Finally, the floor and walls stopped heaving, and she felt that looking up wouldn't cost her a brick to the head.

They were all covered in plaster bits.

Snickers, whose eyelashes were crusted in white dust, started coughing. Rhiannon tugged the neck of the child's dress up to cover her mouth and nose.

"That wasn't an earthquake," she called to Stupid, who had stirred from his spot on the other side of the caved-in hallway.

"Nope," he answered.

The crack that ran down the outer wall and across the floor revealed that day had dawned.

Something big cracked and fell with a boom nearby.

"Looks like time to get out of the building." Stupid halfheartedly brushed off his jeans and carefully stepped toward the gaping hole in the hallway that now separated them from each other.

Two huge floor beams ran the length of either side of the hole, so both sides were fairly safe for now... she hoped.

She glanced back the way they'd come.

"We won't be the only ones with that idea," she said.

Stupid was on the exit side, while it seemed she and Snickers were trapped on the still-connected-to-the-bad-guys' side.

"Can you clear some of that debris?" She indicated Stupid's side. It was a smallish hole, after all, not that she was good with measurements.

Snickers just gaped at her as she twisted the back of the child's dress into two fistfuls to make two handles.

"Trust me, baby," she whispered, and then kissed her forehead.

She prayed to a God she didn't believe in and then tossed Snickers across the hole.

Stupid, waiting, fell as he caught Snickers on the other side.

Then as Stupid and Snickers found footing, Rhiannon took a few steps back and eyed up the gap while she knotted her long dress around her waist.

Snickers stared at her with soul-choked eyes.

"It's okay; I've made jumps twice this," she soothed. *With wires*, an inner voice reminded her.

Then she looked at Stupid, whose ever-present unhurriedness seemed to have deserted him.

"You'll make sure Snickers gets to Will?" she asked.

The child's body stiffened at this question, and she was sorry to frighten her but felt she had to ask the favor of Stupid, just in case.

Stupid shook his head. "It's a package deal. I need to get both of you out, or Tex'll have my head."

She laughed and then tried for a teasing tone for Snickers's benefit, "He's not getting rid of me that easy. I just might be a step behind."

She ran, jumped, and knew milliseconds into the leap that she hadn't put enough behind it. She'd been running on empty for days.

Still, she flung her arms forward in a final attempt to snag the broken floorboards on the far side.

Stupid's fingers brushed her forearms.

Jagged wood speared her chest and belly, and, as she slid downward, ripped through the front of her dress.

Stupid couldn't get a grip on her.

Rhiannon was wrong about that beam being solid, and it cracked under her added weight. She was afraid that the entire floor would come down on her.

She fell. Maybe it was a twelve- or fifteen-foot drop to

the next floor, where she thankfully landed on her feet, knees slightly bent, and then on her ass.

She looked up to see Snickers on her knees, peering down. The child's tension eased when she offered up a smile. Stupid looked down too.

"I'll find rope," Stupid offered, already on his way.

"No," she called to bring him back. "The floor looks solid down here. We'll meet in the next stairwell, just keep heading east."

He nodded and, tugging a very reluctant Snickers with him, quickly took off in that direction. The stairwell was probably the safest place to be right now.

Rhiannon sat there among the debris; her body was still absorbing the fall, and she was in no hurry to find out if she had sustained further injury. She might be in a little shock, but despite that, she was really sure that was a nail sticking out of her foot. A very rusty, now bloody, nail.

She finally convinced herself to pull the nail out and get moving. Ripping a bandage from the dress skirt had been oddly difficult.

She kept to the edges of the hall, guessing that the floor was more secure there, but she still managed to move at a fairly quick pace.

She made it to the stairwell, wrenched the slightly buckled steel door open with some effort, and wedged herself through to the inside.

Snickers and Stupid were not waiting.

Despite her gut-twist instinct to do so, she didn't call out; she didn't want to draw attention to them.

A few steps upward and she quickly figured out the problem. A good chunk of the upper stairs was warped and broken, too dangerous to climb.

Were they waiting for her here, or had they back-tracked? They might have gone up a floor to see if they could backtrack that way...

"Clarence?" she called, remembering to use his given name.

"Rhiannon!" Stupid's relieved voice floated down. They were only a few feet away.

"Can you go back?" she asked.

"Better to find rope, pull you up or jump down, don't ya think?"

"The floor isn't stable," she said. "We pick a rendezvous point that we can both get to safely, and go our separate ways till then."

"A what?" he asked, and she felt bad about the chagrin she heard in his voice.

"A meeting spot."

"Okay then," he answered and then fell silent.

"Stupid fuck! You know the area, you pick a spot!" she yelled.

"Right... ummm... we both get out of the building, that seems smart." He pondered while she willed herself not to scream at him again and again.

" 'Kay, how about a coffee shop, one of those Star-bucks?" he finally offered. "There's one on the northeast corner. You go down a level, head left, but it'll take us a bit longer."

"Perfect, I'll wait for you there." Not great directions, but how hard could a coffee shop be to find?

She swiveled to run down the stairs and found that a man had been standing right behind her the entire length of the conversation.

He wasn't armed, though.

Unless you counted the meaty paws that were currently stretched to clench either side of the stair railing and effectively block her exit.

"Be safe," Stupid called.

Rhiannon swallowed her fear and answered in a steady voice. "You too."

Then she smashed her foot into Meat's face.

With shoes, this move would have done more than just bruise his already flat nose. Unfortunately, he got one of his paws around her ankle and pulled.

She blacked out for a bit — your head hitting a concrete stair will do that to you — but when she woke, she was slung over Meat's shoulder.

Her bruised or maybe broken ribs didn't fancy this position; and, realizing she was awake, Meat jumped to smash those tender ribs into his shoulder.

The resulting wash of pain caused her to black out again.

She didn't even scream first.

When she next awoke, she was splayed out on a hotel bed; she could tell by the feel of the cheap comforter and lumpy mattress.

Meat loomed.

"Ah, good," he said, and then wrapped one big paw around her neck to pin her while he began to widen the already gaping tears at the front of her dress.

Grit underneath her fingers informed her that plaster covered everything in this room as well. Her tongue was too thick for her mouth.

She ineffectively batted at his head and neck with her hands and arms, but the lack of oxygen didn't help her aim.

He reached down to loosen his pants.

She dimly realized that this nobody was actually going to rape her; something that, no matter what else had happened, she'd managed to avoid.

Her hand hunted the bed, but pillows and blankets weren't going to help.

She felt his belt buckle hit her inner thigh and shoved at his chest.

She couldn't stop the sob that broke through, and that made him grin and give her an extra neck squeeze, almost like a sexy love tap.

He pressed his turgid dick against her, but he'd forgotten her panties and growled in frustration.

He dug in his back pocket and yanked out a small knife.

He leaned back — thereby easing the pressure on her neck but still attempting to keep her thighs pinned — to slip the knife beneath her underwear.

Rhiannon smashed her forehead into his nose.

Already off balance, he stumbled. Nose smashing was quickly becoming a signature move for her.

Unfortunately, the knife went into her thigh as he pulled her with him off the bed.

She wasn't about to be raped by some fucking unknown player; she was the fucking lead in this fucking story.

She grappled for the knife.

Meat tried to gain his feet, but got all tangled in her limbs. He fell on her, and therefore onto the waiting knife, but it took three more stabs to mortally wound him.

Sometime later, Rhiannon was aware of his attempt to climb off her and toward where she thought the door might be, but she was beyond caring.

She slept for a little while.

She was hurt badly enough that she didn't think she'd be getting up. She knew Snickers would find Will, that Stupid would make sure of that.

Will inspired loyalty.

She drifted.

The building rumbled, and some dust or dirt or drywall or plaster tickled her cheek. She hated things touching her face... *bugs... rain...*

She shifted her head in hopes of shaking the dust off her cheek, and the resulting jolt of pain brought her back to painful semi-awareness. She momentarily longed for the bliss of near death... this complacency frightened her into action better than any rallying speech could have.

She shifted again.

Some of her hair was stuck to the carpet with what might be dried blood, and she wondered how long she'd been lying there. Then she really hoped it was her own blood, because the thought of lying in the blood of some would-be dirty rapist made her beyond ill.

So she decided to get up.

She had always been better on her feet than her back anyway — and, ultimately, it was more flattering aesthetically. Plus, Snickers would insist on looking for her, and the child didn't need to find her dead by some guy with his ass exposed to the rafters.

Something squawked, and she momentarily thought a crow

was attacking her, though she found she wasn't concerned about how a bird would have gotten inside ...

By the second squawk, she realized she was hearing a two-way radio attached to the dead rapist's belt, which was currently around his knees. Would-Be-Rapist, which was a better name than Meat, must have turned down the volume so as to not be disturbed when stalking and raping her.

The radio squawked again as she reached to retrieve it. An unsexed voice, oddly quiet, screamed bloody, terrified murder on the other end.

Supposedly the city was under attack: an army on the main street, gunfire, and, "What were they to do? Why wasn't anyone picking up at H.Q.?"

No one to answer your call, dumb-ass, she thought about replying, but then decided that Radio-Voice had never done anything to deserve her lip.

The building rumbled again; the walls creaked, and she decided the source of the boom seemed farther away now. Not a bomb or earthquake.

She almost tossed the radio, but then thought better of it.

Her throat killed. *What was it with assholes and strangling?* This wasn't the first time some guy tried to wrap his hands around her neck. She wondered if she could even talk, but felt too raw and bruised to attempt a test. Even an involuntary moan hurt her something nasty.

She realized, even after deciding to stand, that she'd been crawling around.

Her dress was shredded.

She attempted to stand.

It didn't go well.

She'd lost her shoes but didn't worry about it when she recalled where she'd left them behind — one buried in the Boss's neck — *though maybe not anymore?* She wondered if she had short-term memory loss. Maybe she'd be lucky and only lose all the bad memories. This made her think of Will.

Suddenly, she had a feeling that if she only got Snickers back to Will and he forgave her for ... *Well, maybe the bad shit wouldn't matter.* Actually, thought of in that light, maybe the bad shit never did matter ...

She was standing, unaware of how she came to be on her feet and how long she'd been on them.

She stood swaying in the middle of the room.

She took a couple of steps, found them easier than she'd anticipated, and so she took a few more.

Something was dragging behind her, though.

She turned her head as little as she could and saw that half of her dress, ripped and heavy with blood, was leaving a red trail as she moved.

So she ripped the rest of it off, mourning the lovely fabric only slightly as she tossed it away. *Never could get blood out of silk anyway.*

She was a little bit pleased that Would-Be-Rapist had gotten his pants down, and not just because pawing at his dick had distracted him. She didn't have to move him much to steal his pants, and with the help of his belt, those jeans fit better than they should have.

She sneered at the idea that some scrawny-legged asshole with weird meaty hands had thought he could take anything from her. He hadn't gotten her body or life, and she was fucked if she'd give him her future.

Thus, she rallied to move with the pain instead of despite it.

First, before redressing, she remembered to bind the knife wound on her thigh; seemed like stemming the blood loss was a good idea.

Then she clasped the radio to Would-Be-Rapist's belt and stepped over his corpse to once again find Snickers, freedom, and her future.

Storming a city was pretty much what it sounded like, though perhaps a little more organized; no disrespect to Mother Nature intended.

He had only blacked out for a few minutes, but it felt like hours to his exhausted system. And although according to Rav, he'd lost quite a bit of blood, Will actually felt rejuvenated by the involuntary nap. The encounter itself served to reinforce his drive to protect the people he would like to consider his future, his family.

So they made it over the bridge and, in a few miles, hit clear sailing on the highway to the city. It was kind of someone to have cleared it. Course, they then figured out where all the cars were: piled at the mouths of two of the three bridges they tried to use to access downtown.

So One Ear's map had been accurate, and he had wasted precious time not trusting it.

At the Burrard Street Bridge, they found the first resistance, but once they regrouped with the tank out front, the bad guys ceased fire quickly.

A mortar shot convinced the defenders that mere

bullets couldn't stop the invasion. Will was relieved the tank could still fire after his tunnel stunt.

They actually laid down their arms, walked out of their outposts and surrendered, often smiling and laughing, which baffled him even further.

Why shoot at them in the first place, only to surrender, smiling, when they figured they were up against a superior force?

Later, he found out Big's rhetoric had preceded them.

Course, that was exactly what he had asked them to do via the bullhorn. But still, he was surprised at the token resistance.

Why follow the so-called Boss in the first place?

They got over this bridge and soon realized they'd invaded a city in the middle of a civil war.

Red Jackets seemed pretty willing to kill anyone.

They, or the Resistance as Big was calling them, lost men.

They refused to leave their wounded or dead behind. Men were assigned to carry these few back to waiting flatbeds. Course, those men often got wounded in their rescue attempts. They were really going to need a doctor, better sooner than later.

The tank spoke a few more times. Boomer angled as high as he could and took out the tops of buildings, hoping that people chose to hide lower.

It was difficult to argue with a tank, and after an endless

stretch of time — ten minutes in actuality — even the Red Jackets began to surrender.

Among them was a doctor, who they immediately put to work tending the wounded as they continued to carve their way deeper into the city.

While bullets flew and the tank tore through asphalt, Will calmly dictated terms via bullhorn.

He offered amnesty, freedom, and choice.

He never thought to just ask for Rhiannon or Snickers. That would've been too simple; later, he understood it also would've probably worked.

She made it out to the street only to retreat into the very next doorway. She wasn't getting between gun-firing Red Jackets and their targets.

Also, it soon became apparent just by rotating her aching head 180 degrees that the fucking city was littered with fucking Starbucks. She saw two across from each other in the next intersection and another sign one and a half blocks west as well.

Lacking energy to the nth degree while trying to dissect what she understood of Stupid's thought process and having no understanding which way was north, Rhiannon chose the coffee shop closest to her. But one corner of it — the corner that had most likely held the glass entrance — was crumpled. She'd have to figure out if there was an interior entrance.

She glanced back at the hotel. It was definitely broken into three slumped pieces. The Red Jackets must have tracked her there, and when they got a location but not an exact room, decided a bomb or three was a precise enough weapon.

Interestingly, they hadn't given a shit that she and Snickers might have still been in the building. She'd make sure to remember that slight.

She zigzagged across the street, dodging cars, crumpled pavement, and — oddly — jellybeans, to the entrance of the building that had held the coffee shop.

Fortunately, no one shot at her.

Unfortunately, she moved slowly enough they could've easily hit her. She hoped there was an energy drink waiting for her at Starbucks. In passing, she noted the candy shop next door, which explained, sort of, the jellybeans.

The front door gaped, which made her life a little easier, and she picked through debris toward where she thought the rear entrance to the coffee shop might be. She guessed this was some sort of a bank, back when money had meant everything and before it had crumbled in the bomb aftershock.

She had to climb over a broken wall to find the Starbucks, but her sense of direction hadn't failed her despite the building being half destroyed.

A massive round of gunfire bursted out from what seemed like a few blocks away, and the building threatened to crumble after another explosion.

What glass remained unbroken promptly broke, and Rhiannon took the moment to shield herself. Then she looked around the coffee shop.

No Snickers.

But then not even Stupid was stupid enough to hang out in the middle of some room just waiting for trouble. At least she hoped he wasn't.

A noise came from a room behind what used to be the front counter, and she strained to hear what she thought might be soft sobbing.

She tried to arm herself with a chunk of countertop, but decided the granite — which was oddly upscale for a coffee place — was too heavy. She opted for a chair leg instead.

She moved toward the back room, perhaps an office/change area. She pushed open the door, but it took a moment for her brain to interpret the sight before her.

A pudgy — or rather, a puffy, mushy — man leaned over another man, who she recognized as Grunt. The first man seemed to be trying to resuscitate Grunt. Then she realized the mound of mush was actually eating Grunt's neck, which was impossibly twisted. Grunt's vacant eyes furthered her theory.

Mandy was balled under a desk and sobbing into her hands like some pathetic moron; even with the Infected blocking the door, she could have fought.

"You're a moron, Mandy," Rhiannon blurted. That got Mandy's attention, though not the Infected's.

It, taking one kill at a time, kept its focus on Grunt's flesh.

She needed a sturdier weapon; a chair leg couldn't do much damage without a lot of strength behind it, and she didn't have any in reserve.

"Fuck, Grunt's gun is lying right there, you idiotic bitch." She indicated the 9mm between Mandy and the dining Infected.

Mandy just returned to sobbing.

Rhiannon wasn't vaulting over some monster to grab a gun to save a fucking imbecile who wouldn't even try to save herself when a gun was in reach.

She actually turned to leave, but the Infected lunged for her; seemed it had noticed her and didn't want its prey to wander off.

She fell backwards through the doorway.

It pulled her back inside, but not before it gave her feet a sniff and actually licked one of them: the one crusty with blood from the nail.

She repositioned her makeshift weapon so she could stab it through an eye or something.

Then, out of somewhere, Stupid hollered a war cry, leaped over her, and chopped off the Infected's head in the completion of his lunge.

He paused to look at her, said, "Sorry; had to get an axe," and then entered the office.

She stood in time to see him chop off Grunt's head.

Mandy shrieked and — *finally* — went for the gun, but Stupid reached down to easily pluck it from her hands.

Then he turned his back on Mandy and reached out a helping hand to steady Rhiannon, as she was still a little wobbly on her feet.

Grunt's head was slowing its bloody spin.

"Don't think their victims reanimate like zombies, Clarence," she commented.

Stupid shrugged. "Better safe than sorry, hey?"

"Guess so," she, still quite woozy, agreed.

Snickers darted from her hiding spot and wrapped her leg in a hug.

"We didn't recognize you right away." Stupid eyed her apologetically.

She nodded but didn't fill him in on the details. There was sure to be enough bruising and blood to tell her story visually anyway.

"There seems to be a war going on out there," she said to Stupid as he handed her a couple of his extra guns.

"Yup." He grinned.

Mandy wandered out and started to try to fix a pot of coffee.

Snickers eyed Mandy distrustfully and held on to the gun tied around her neck. Rhiannon eyed this gun necklace and glared at Stupid, who just shrugged.

"Street ain't safe," he offered instead. "Best keep to the buildings."

She wasn't totally sure that was completely logical, but light-headed from blood loss, she was more than ready for someone else to steer.

"I know a way," Mandy murmured, as she oddly and regimentally tamped espresso. *Perhaps she'd been hit a little too hard on the head?*

Unfortunately, Stupid looked interested in Mandy's version of insanity.

"This bitch tried to sell us into slavery," Rhiannon sneered.

That didn't seem to dissuade Stupid. He eyed Mandy's red-painted jacket and then decided. "She'll know the city, then, and its secret passageways."

Rhiannon wasn't too sure what novel he got the passageway notion from, and maybe he didn't even read, but following Mandy was a bad idea.

Though seeing as she didn't currently have a better idea, she thought she'd tag along until an opportunity arose, because one always did.

Stupid relieved her of her radio and started to try to contact someone on it, but it had a pretty short range. He kept trying anyway. Snickers filled her new backpack with water and stale packaged cookies.

Mandy led them through hallways, alleys, and multiple doorways. Sometimes they seemed to be below ground and at other times not so much.

Once, they entered a department store via one of those overhead glassed walkways. In the near distance, smoke rose up from the burning city.

Rhiannon took the opportunity as they walked by to grab a T-shirt to replace the remains of the silk dress she'd wrapped around her torso. She also grabbed jeans for Snickers, who pulled them on under her dress as they continued to jog after Mandy. She didn't see shoes, though.

At all times, Mandy headed southeasterly; it felt right, so they let her lead. Unfortunately, that was also closer to the explosions.

Occasional windows revealed that a herd of the Infected, probably from the parking garage, had now joined the war.

They ate anyone they could grab, regardless of political affiliation.

Mandy eventually led them to what might have once been a private gym of sorts. Rhiannon snagged a few sure-to-be-stale PowerBars for her and Snickers.

As they turned into a connecting hallway, she slowed her pace while Mandy quickened hers to a jog. This hall looked dreadfully familiar.

Mandy darted through a far door.

Stupid yelled, "Hey, wait up!" and started to follow.

Rhiannon grabbed his arm and he stilled at her touch.

"What is it?" Stupid asked, and all the while his eyes darted around in search of immediate danger.

She was very aware of Snickers hanging off her arm.

"This place..." she started to say, but then didn't know how to articulate the feeling. "I ... I think I've been here ... before ... it isn't good."

A sharp scream emanated from Mandy's general direction and was quickly followed by waves and waves of keening.

The hair stood up on her arms.

"Mandy isn't leading us out. She's led us farther in." Despite her mounting horror, Rhiannon started to step closer and closer to the doors.

Snickers held her back.

"We leave," Stupid decided. "She's on her own."

She continued to move almost unwillingly forward, not wanting to, but —

Through the doors, she could see into what was once a series of racquetball courts. Except now, now each court was filled with medical stuff — *monitors, machines, equipment — whatever the hell all that shit was called.*

Each hospital bed was occupied by a woman. The woman in the first bed was hooked to a bunch of machines, strapped down, and recently dead. The woman's — or rather, the *patient's, or the prisoner's* — throat had been slit. Even with her head cranked back, her blood had soaked downward across her chest and bed to drip onto the floor.

A whimper broke through Rhiannon's frozen, terrified stare. She tore her eyes from the dead woman and, despite the protest of her ribs, snatched up Snickers in her arms.

Stupid sprang forward and quickly entered the racquetball court to check on the woman, but it was more than apparent she was beyond rescue. He moaned just once, like he was briefly voicing a heavy wound.

Snickers kept trying to see what was going on, and Rhiannon pleaded with her, "Please close your eyes, baby, you don't need to see this, please. You never need this."

But Snickers seemed scared to close her eyes.

Stupid turned his head away from the dead woman and sought them out, like he was desperate to lay eyes on something alive.

"You know her, Clarence?" she found herself asking, even though she didn't want to converse.

"She looks like someone ... her sister maybe. Big's lady. I ... I don't think ... we'll have to leave her." Stupid's words tumbled about as he tried to process the scene. She didn't know how to respond, so he relieved her of that burden as he dashed over to the next racquet court; but the woman in there, who might have actually been pregnant, was also dead.

The keening ahead settled into broken sobs. Mandy had led them to the baby mills, where someone had been recently, methodically sacrificing the breeders.

Rhiannon followed Stupid down the hall as he darted from court to court. She knew looking for survivors was the right thing to do, but was utterly terrified by the thought that she'd almost been trapped here herself.

She had to lower Snickers, as she couldn't carry her much longer. She grasped both of the child's hands and kneeled for better eye contact.

"You look at me. Don't look anywhere but me. I'll keep you safe, always."

Snickers nodded and raised her hand to suck her thumb. With a heavy heart, she pulled the thumb from the child's mouth, like Will would have. Then she straightened to help Stupid search.

When they reached Mandy about five courts later, they hadn't found anyone alive. The body Mandy was keening over didn't help that total.

Stupid tried to tug Mandy away from the dead woman, who looked enough like Mandy — though younger and without the red paint — to be her sister. Mandy turned on Stupid, screaming over and over and beating his chest. "It was all for nothing, all for nothing, nothing, nothing."

Rhiannon tugged Snickers away into the hall while Stupid struggled to calm Mandy.

She felt the child stiffen beside her and followed her gaze up the hallway.

There at the end of the courts stood the Boss, bloody knife and all.

She screamed at him, not knowing why that was her first response.

She raised her gun, but out of the corner of her eye she saw Snickers do the same; that gave her pause and quick doubt that more killing was the best option. The fact that the child held a gun at all made her heart tighten.

Stupid, followed by Mandy, blew by them to give chase.

The Boss, who was probably currently out of bullet range anyway, turned heel and ran.

Snickers moved as if to follow, but Rhiannon held her back.

She had heard something.

She tapped her ear, and the child tilted her head to listen.

There.

A weak cry.

They ran to the court that the Boss had been about to

enter, and found a too-young-to-be-so-very-pregnant teen trying to get free from the machines in which she was tangled.

She and Snickers dashed in and with some effort, a couple of knives, and grateful sobbing on the teen's part, managed to get her unstrapped.

She offered the teen, who had managed to sit up, some of the water they'd collected earlier.

The teen gulped it and then offered her name, "Chéri."

"I'm Rhiannon and this is Snickers," she introduced.

"I know who you are," Chéri said neutrally, and then turned to beam at Snickers. "That's a great name. I haven't seen someone your age in a long time. I am glad you are here to rescue me."

Snickers nodded shyly.

"The others?" Chéri asked quietly as she tried out her legs.

"All gone, I think," she answered just as quietly, "but we still need to check."

Stupid, wheezing, flung himself through the door.

Chéri stumbled back against the bed, protectively clutching her very engorged belly.

"Didn't want to leave you long. Mandy kept after him." He tried to breathe and speak at the same time, all the while eyeing Chéri distrustfully.

"This is Clarence; he's with us," Rhiannon explained.

Chéri recovered enough to wrap herself, over the hospital gown, in a sheet, toga-style.

"Clarence, we need to —" Rhiannon started, but Stupid figured what she needed.

"Got it." He proceeded to check the other courts for survivors.

There weren't any.

The Boss, perhaps unable to guarantee keeping them to himself, had slaughtered his entire forced harem and their unborn children, save for Chéri.

The loss was devastating, but they didn't have time to mourn. It was time to get the hell out of here and home to Will.

She took the lead.

Stupid reluctantly stayed with Chéri, who seemed ready to give birth any minute. He had wanted point, but Rhiannon couldn't support Chéri and take care of Snickers.

Combined, Stupid and Chéri moved slowly enough that she and Snickers were the first to step out into the war and gunfire and terror of the street.

The city burned — or at least the long blocks running from the ocean to the river seemed to be in the process of destruction.

She didn't know which way to turn. Smoke billowed and curled from multiple directions; people darted around, but the shooting had stopped.

She tugged Snickers's dress up over her mouth again, and the child pressed against her leg and hip as she tried to determine which way to go.

Low rumbling came from the south, or at least what she thought was south. She was all turned about, so she decided to wait for Stupid and Chéri.

Scared to lose Snickers in this false fog, she hitched the

child up on her hip. If she leaned against the doorway, she could support her, for a little while at least.

Then she heard the barking.

A drift of wind cleared the smoke momentarily, and Will, armed to the teeth and covered in protective gear, stepped through.

Flanked by B.B. and about a dozen other very armed men, he was yelling something about putting down the Infected and refuge and freedom.

Someone — who was later introduced as Big — rode behind in a Jeep and echoed these orders via bullhorn.

People actually seemed to be listening.

She stumbled a few steps out from the doorway and immediately drew Will's eye.

He smiled.

The source of the rumble, revealing itself as a tank slowly following behind Will, broke through the smoke.

He brought a tank to rescue them.

She'd never had someone bring a tank to her rescue before, not even in a movie.

Snickers smoothed her cheeks, and Rhiannon realized she was crying joyful tears, a type she didn't even know she was capable of.

Now B.B. had seen them, and the dog barked a greeting.

Then Snickers was out of her arms and running for Will. She blew by B.B., who was also running.

Will flipped his gun behind his back and opened his arms to Snickers. The momentum of her run almost unbalanced him; he hugged the child fiercely.

B.B. dashed to Rhiannon's side and, after getting a head and chest rub, turned to go back to Will. She still hesitated to follow. She didn't know if Will would welcome her after all this —

He looked for her then, over Snickers's shoulder, and was surprised to see her still near the door. His face was streaked with ash and sweat.

Then she too was running and falling into his arms.

She kissed him like she'd never kissed anyone before, like she couldn't even remember or care about all the years of perfected technique. She crushed Snickers between them, but the child didn't complain; she just twisted her hands in the hair at the back of both of their heads.

Will tasted like sweat and a little sweet, maybe like strawberries. He held her hard enough to hurt, but she never wanted him to lessen his grip.

She'd been so lost and floundering, but hadn't even understood she was surrounded by darkness, didn't perceive it until she saw Will's light.

All these years she'd worried about losing herself within someone, and now she, surrounded by fire, bullets and death, had found her home.

The tank rumbled by.

An armed group had formed around them, protecting them as they stupidly, amazingly, continued to kiss in the street.

She pulled back to say the most truthful words she'd ever uttered. "I love you, Will. You and Snickers. I'll never leave you again."

"Rhiannon." He laughed, and she heard her joy reflected back. "Without you there is no future, no reason to be... with you, I hope... I wish... for all of eternity together."

So they kissed again, and she would swear that a cheer rose up from the surrounding army.

Then, oddly, something stung Rhiannon's back, and suddenly Will wasn't kissing her anymore. Her legs went weak and he lowered her to the ground.

Things got a bit blurry and it was hard to breathe. Will kept pulling Snickers, who seemed frantic, off her while he yelled for a doctor.

Everyone else was shouting, and B.B. growled like she was about to rip a throat out. Then she felt the warmth, maybe blood, flooding her back.

Her left lung burned.

Fog drifted in, and then the Red Jacket doctor leaned over her. She tried to fight him off, but Will held her hands.

She pieced together the debate that was going on over her head.

Mandy had shot her from behind.

Stupid, who she found out later had mistakenly let Mandy near enough to hit her target, wanted the traitorous bitch put down.

The doctor, while seeming to patch her up, pleaded for Mandy's life, and Big seemed to be listening to him.

They bargained and argued.

No one wanted to be responsible for Mandy, who — if she turned her head to see — was on the ground a few feet away with Big's boot on her back. There was some talk by the doctor and Big of Mandy being female, and all the death they had already caused, but violence was the theme of the day. Its chaotic energy gave body to the wind that encouraged the fire and smoke rather than dampening it.

Just as Big lowered his gun for a kill shot, Rhiannon found her voice. "No. Let the bitch live. It'll hurt her more to see me happy." Grayness edged her vision, but from the loathing look on Mandy's face, she'd been right about denying her suicide by capital punishment.

Stupid stepped up. He took responsibility for keeping Mandy and attempting to rehabilitate her. He thought it was all his fault, that he should have been more careful —

"Unless Rhiannon dies, Clarence. Then Mandy dies by my hand." Will's chest rumbled as he reluctantly agreed to Stupid's request, and Rhiannon realized he was carrying her somewhere.

She finally focused enough to see Snickers hanging off Will's back like a monkey. Their desperation eased when they saw her eyes open.

She smiled and thought she'd happily die here, even surrounded by death and war and grief.

She'd found her piece of peace.

"Will? Do you believe in true love, then?" she whispered.

"At first sight," he replied in that solid, dependable, utterly truthful way of his.

Of course, dying wasn't really an option when she still had Shotgun Asshole to deal with. She was pretty sure she'd spotted him in the crowd.

SO HE'D WON THE WAR AND FOUND THE GIRLS, only to be sitting by a hospital bed, watching Rhiannon slowly, burning from the inside out, die.

The doctor seemed to think he was being extreme, but everything about Rhiannon was alive and vibrant, and he could see her essence slipping away.

The doctor thought she had an infection, and this confused him for a while, as the bullet wound was so fresh, but then he found the nail hole.

A rusty nail in her foot! What had she been thinking, wandering around in no shoes?

He felt like sobbing, but couldn't for Snickers's sake.

They'd tried to take Snickers away, to eat or sleep, but she refused. At least she'd let Will bathe her face after they'd washed Rhiannon.

The doctor said to let the antibiotics kick in, but Will knew after three days that those pills might be expired even if the doctor said otherwise.

People — Stupid, Big, and the pregnant teen, Chéri, he'd seen with Rhiannon — would periodically hover by the door, but he usually ignored them. Sometimes he had to step out to speak with Big about the city occupation and whatnot, but he felt guilty every time he left Rhiannon's side.

The hospital held a lot of other wounded, and as the days stretched, Will noticed more and more unfamiliar faces in the doorway.

Usually, Stupid and B.B. kept everyone at bay. He wasn't sure what Stupid had done with Mandy, but he appreciated the guard.

On the morning of the third day, Chéri gave birth to a very loud but healthy baby boy. This wasn't as joyful as it should have been. There was some question about whether the virus was still active and whether or not immunity would transfer from parent to child; it hadn't before, but perhaps two immune parents would make a difference. Whether or not he was the father, they never did find the Boss. Before Stupid had locked her away, Mandy hadn't been forthcoming. In fact, she'd adopted a close to catatonic state, but maybe the Boss had died by her hand. They combed the city to verify that 'maybe,' because Will had decided he didn't trust maybes anymore.

Then he started planning.

When night fell and he was pretty sure Rhiannon's fever was high enough to be boiling her brain, he asked Big for a Jeep.

The doctor protested him moving Rhiannon, but there was no ice to be found and, with the hospital at capacity, no energy to spare to make any. Plus, he was tired of helplessly, uselessly waiting.

The doctor fretted about shocking Rhiannon's heart, but Will remembered his mom put him in an ice bath when he was young, so he didn't listen.

Moms often knew better than doctors anyway.

He climbed into the back of the Jeep with Rhiannon in his arms and Snickers and B.B. at his side. He asked Big to drive them to the ocean.

They got as close as they could and he walked the remainder of the way, over the seawall and into the sea. Waves threatened to topple him.

He lost the fight to keep Snickers on shore; he was afraid she'd drown with him needing both arms to hold Rhiannon on the surface. But the child had thrown her gun away and used its necklace to anchor herself to his arm.

At about waist deep, he turned his back to the harbor — at least that was what he thought loomed behind him — and lowered Rhiannon into the water.

Waves broke on his back and he looked up to see what had to be hundreds of flashlights trained on him.

B.B. still stood guard on the shore.

The rustling and voices he'd heard in the park hadn't been the wind as he'd absentmindedly assumed, but people following them from the city.

A wave crashed over his back, and Snickers clung to his arm. He floated Rhiannon and realized her white night-gown must glow in the lit water.

He made out murmurs and then a tune.

They were singing.

It spread through the crowd. Some kneeled, some swayed, but they all sang. He recognized the song from Sunday school, and his heart constricted painfully.

Gloria in excelsis Deo;
Gloria in excelsis Deo.

They sang hymn after hymn.

Heat radiated off Rhiannon.

Snickers shivered. He wondered if it was insane to risk the child's health like this, but as he dragged his eyes from the crowd, he found Rhiannon looking at him.

"I'm wet," she whispered. "Is this payback for the toilet flush?"

He didn't know what to answer, or what he was feeling, so he just laughed.

Rhiannon raised her hand from the water and placed it on his cheek. It was cold. Thank God it was cold. Her fever had broken.

The crowd switched hymns to "Morning Has Broken."

Will found his voice. "I've finally woken up only to find that I am at the start of the end of the world." He'd been thinking about that for a while.

"The world hasn't ended... people have died, but the world certainly doesn't need people, except you and Snickers," Rhiannon replied.

"There is always going to be someone with a bigger tank... what if the chaos never stops, what if I can't keep you safe?"

"We'll worry about those assholes when we see their

rifle sights; till then, we've a daughter to raise and a world to resurrect."

Then she curled her head into his chest and he brought her out of the water, out of their witnessed baptism and into the rest of their life.

And it helped, long term, that this incident raised them to a mythical status... as long as he didn't hear any stories about him walking on water.

THEY MADE IT THROUGH.

Was there any doubt? It was their story after all. They figured out the happy ending.

She had scars that would stay with her for the rest of her life, that she wouldn't trade for anything before or after the virus.

They went home.

A group of people stayed in the city, but many, including the doctor, Chéri, Rav, and Boomer, had come back with them. Chéri's baby was a boy — named after Will, of course — though Rhiannon quickly, and with only a touch of irony, nicknamed him Atlas. The first of his generation, which was either a terrible or joyful burden, she couldn't decide.

Before they'd left, they formed a council — not elected, democracy had to wait — but twelve good people would decide how this part of the world should run.

Big stayed to oversee the day-to-day of the city, guided by Will, who was regarded as a king of sorts. Stupid, because of Mandy, stayed too, but they'd all visit.

She never did get her hands on Shotgun Asshole — or One Ear — as Will called him, but she found she was becoming rather patient in her middle age.

They'd returned about a week ago. She found the poor strawberry plant, still on the kitchen table and root-bound, and immediately planted it.

She watched Will's big hands slicing tomatoes from Snickers's garden for dinner. Luanne, who'd return to the city with Big, had maintained it.

She remembered how quickly — or rather, eagerly, easily, peacefully — she came every time he laid those rough but tenderly used hands on her.

Snickers wandered into the kitchen to jolt her from her sexy, distracting, and currently inappropriate train of thought.

The child, though she'd really grown, used her stepladder to pull three plates down from the cupboard. She then crossed to the table.

Not knowing why she asked, seeing as it was obvious, Rhiannon said, "Whatcha doing, sweetness?"

"Setting the dinner table," Snickers answered.

Will fumbled with the knife. She momentarily thought he'd sliced his finger off, but it seemed pretty whole when he sucked on it. He turned, surprise etched on his face, to look at Snickers.

"What? That's what families do. Eat dinner together, don't they?" Snickers said.

Will took his finger from his mouth. "Don't forget

spoons; Rhiannon likes to use one with spaghetti," he, so casual, told the girl.

"I know," Snickers grumbled; but then, very willingly, she added cutlery and then napkins to the table. She even added flowers from her garden.

Will returned to slicing the tomatoes, but his hands were shaking. Rhiannon laid her hand on his chest. She could feel his heart pounding. She gently nudged him to the side and took over slicing.

Snickers folded the napkins into fans.

Finally, Will whispered, "She's okay."

RHIANNON FLASHED HER MILLION-DOLLAR SMILE at him, the one that made his belly drop, the one he knew he'd carry with him through death. Though hopefully not before he saw it duplicated on their children's faces.

"With you, everyone is always okay, Will. How could we not be? You make it so." Rhiannon spoke in a way that made him believe the outrageous.

THEY WERE KISSING AGAIN.

Not that it really bothered her, but the tomatoes were going to get crushed. Dinner wasn't going to make itself.

She added water glasses to the table and remembered another table and another family, but those thoughts were always fuzzy and faraway in her head.

They — Rhiannon and Will — kissed like they belonged on the TV. They were just all full of color and always the brightest thing in any room.

It was easy to love them best, and B.B., of course. She knew they worried about her, but she figured that was their job now.

Rhiannon laughed that soft sound she made when she was really happy; then Will laughed loudly like he did even when no one had told a joke.

Rhiannon offered her a slice of carrot and she ate it. She liked it when Rhiannon fed her, even though she wasn't a baby anymore.

Rhiannon was better at cooking, but sucked at math. Will taught the science stuff. She figured out that cooking and gardening were more important than science and math, but she didn't want to hurt Will's feelings, so she let him teach her fractions and all that other number stuff.

Rhiannon was dancing and humming again while she cooked, and Will always watched her like he couldn't look anywhere but at Rhiannon.

She was secretly surprised that Rhiannon didn't dance very well; she seemed to try to make her own beat despite what the music said. Will had put on some Paul Simon songs again, which always reminded her of trips in the truck. He encouraged Rhiannon and tried to join in. She figured it was okay that Rhiannon was bad at dancing and math. That it kind of evened everything out for all the normal people.

Like that boy who'd been following her around lately.

So what if we both have dogs and are kind of the same age? Eight is so NOT nine!

That boy was so normal he was boring; he'd never even shot a gun, and he'd never rescued someone like she had.

She was a hero.

And she had decided she totally liked the name Snickers way more than Laurie anyway.

ACKNOWLEDGMENTS

For Michael
without whom there would be no love stories

With thanks to:

<u>Editor</u>
Scott Fitzgerald Gray

<u>My proofreaders</u>
Pauline Nolet & Diana Cox

<u>My beta readers</u>
Ita Margalit, David Spencer, Heather Doidge-Sidhu, Clare
Hodge & Pam Kearns

<u>For their continual encouragement, feedback & general
advice</u>
Eric Finkel, Scott Fitzgerald Gray, Michelle Demers & Ian
Alexander Martin

ABOUT THE AUTHOR

Meghan Ciana Doidge is an award-winning writer based out of Vancouver, British Columbia, Canada. She has a penchant for bloody love stories, superheroes, and the supernatural. She also has a thing for chocolate, potatoes, and cashmere.

For recipes, giveaways, news, and glimpses of upcoming stories, please connect with Meghan via:
www.madebymeghan.ca
info@madebymeghan.ca

facebook.com/MeghanCianaDoidge
instagram.com/meghancianadoidge
tiktok.com/@meghancianadoidge

Instincts and Impostors (Amplifier 5)

Endings and Empathy (Amplifier 6)

Misplaced Souls (Misfits 1)

Awakening Infinity (Archivist 0)

Invoking Infinity (Archivist 1)

Compelling Infinity (Archivist 2)

Awry (Conduit 1)

Grand Romantic Delusions and the Madness of Mirth (Part 1 & 2)

Snag (Conduit 2)

Novellas/Shorts

Love Lies Bleeding

The Graveyard Kiss (Reconstructionist 0.5)

Dawn Bytes (Reconstructionist 1.5)

An Uncut Key (Reconstructionist 2.5)

Graveyards, Visions, and Other Things that Byte (Dowser 8.5)

The Amplifier Protocol (Amplifier 0)

Close to Home (Amplifier 0.5)

The Music Box (Amplifier 4.5)

Moments of the Adept Universe 1

Recon Mission: Bee (Amplifier 5.5)

Soulmates, Doorways, and Other Unruly Magic (Dowser 9.5)